A TASTE
OF DEATH

A TASTE
OF DEATH

•

Mary Ellen Hughes

AVALON BOOKS
NEW YORK

APR 1 0 2003

IN MEMORIAM

Gertrude Gustad Lemanski
(1909-1989)

Mom, whose love of reading, especially mysteries,
always inspired me.

Acknowledgments

Special thanks to my family—husband Terry, Stephen Hughes, Suzanne and John Baker, Leanne, Joshua and Jordan Hughes, Barbara Gawronski, Ed and Anita Lemanski, and Ted and Janet Lemanski who all somehow manage to keep me grounded as well as be my greatest cheering section.

Many thanks for the help of the Annapolis critique group: Janet Benrey, Ray Flynt, Trish Marshall, Sherriel Mattingly, Bonnie Settle, Marcia Talley, and Christiane Carlson-Thies who were always generous with encouragement and unflinchingly honest advice.

Thank you also to Kevin Hagerich for graciously sharing his knowledge of hunting and firearms with this novice.

Prologue

The bamboo-like cuttings lay piled on the table next to a yellow, water-filled plastic basin, each matching the others precisely in length, as if that somehow mattered. Rubber-gloved hands picked them up one by one and placed them into the water, pushing them under gently, almost lovingly, leaving them to soak.

A soft voice read aloud from a book propped open nearby, reading slowly, as if savoring each word: "Oleander . . . extremely poisonous . . . heart stimulator . . . immediate reactions . . ."

A chuckle rolled out. "Perfect."

The hands returned to the cuttings and squeezed the leaves tightly, wringing out every possible drop of liquid after removing them from the water. Fingers gripped a small bottle, dipping it into the basin, holding it, tipped, until the excess air bubbled to the top, then capped and wiped it. Steady hands slid the bottle onto a shelf, unlabeled, to sit among similar-sized jars of ordinary spices.

"A fitting place for you to be," the voice said to the innocent-looking bottle in a mocking tone, "since you will add a certain zest to someone's food. Soon."

Chapter One

Maggie Olenski searched through the bag of sourballs in the console of her Chevy Cavalier, pulled one out, and worked the cellophane off with one hand as she drove. Reba McIntyre's voice sang out from the car stereo and Maggie hummed an occasional, somewhat juicy note or two along with her as she savored the taste of tangy cherry, her favorite.

With the winter sun shining brightly through the windshield, warming up the interior, Maggie had long since shrugged out of her parka. She watched the snow piles edging the borders of the Garden State Parkway slowly grow in size as she headed north, the small tingle of excitement down in the pit of her stomach growing along with them. Maggie had left Baltimore behind in the dark, pre-dawn hours that morning and was driving up to ski country.

The most important equipment she had packed that morning, however, were not skis but her laptop computer and printer. Maggie expected to spend several weeks in Cedar Hill, New Hampshire, and, while some skiing was in the picture, she planned to fill most of her time at her computer, writing.

"Maggie, that's great!" she remembered her friend Dyna Hall squealing into the phone, obviously truly happy for her when she heard Maggie had received a contract on her book proposal, a children's math puzzle book. "Why don't you use my folks' cabin up in New Hampshire to work on it? You could have it all to yourself. No distractions. It'd be perfect!"

It had been tempting. Maybe too tempting? Dyna promised there would be no distractions. However, living within reach of ski slopes when you loved to ski could reasonably be called a distraction. But Dyna continued to push it.

"I could come up with you, just long enough to get you settled in, of course. We could take a few runs down the slopes at Big Bear before I take off, so you could pick out your favorite ones for later."

When Maggie protested that she would have to spend her time writing, not skiing, Dyna argued, "But you have to ski, at least a little. The exercise will be good for your brain. You'll have plenty of time to write, but you can't work sixteen hours a day. You'd have to have some fun time. How can you write a fun book for kids when you're not having any fun?"

Dyna's argument had a certain logic to it, Maggie had to admit, a kind of "Dyna" logic, but reasonable. She had mulled it over. With Maggie's boyfriend, Rob, away teaching at a Florida tennis camp, maybe a change of scene would be better. If she stayed in Baltimore she knew she would face many wrenching reminders of his absence simply by driving past places they had frequented together.

Then there was Maggie's mother, beginning to make noises about Maggie possibly helping out at the family bakery, ". . . just once in a while. It's so hard to find good help, and you'll have this free time . . ."

That had tipped the scale.

Maggie knew her mother. Free time, to her, was any time not spent on one's feet and moving. If Maggie was simply sitting at her computer, she was free and could therefore be called on to be more productive. Maggie would never get her book written if she stayed within sight and reach of her mother. She started packing.

It was arranged that Dyna would fly up and meet her at the cabin. Maggie would use some of the ski equipment that the Halls always kept there, thereby saving precious packing space in her car. Maggie would take a few runs with Dyna at Big Bear, and settle down to the serious work of writing her book as soon as she had the place to herself—which was what she looked forward to most of all.

"Solitude, peace and tranquility. It'll be great," Maggie said to herself between hums with Reba, amused at the contradictory excitement the words stirred in her. Solitude and excitement. Maybe it was a weird combination for some, but it worked for her. She could hardly wait.

As the landscape grew steadily whiter during her drive northward, she realized that for most of her life, first as a student, then as a teacher in a school system that seemed to close at the first fall of a snowflake, snow had become equated with days off. And now she was anticipating many, many snow days. A definite plus, but there was also a worrisome side. Taking this time off from teaching was risky. Harvey Braun, her principal, had been less than thrilled with the idea when she broached it to him.

"A leave of absence in the middle of the school year? You're out of your frigging mind!" was how he had charmingly put it. But Maggie had hung in there, managing to discover, through rapid networking, an available teacher newly moved into the area and looking for a few months' work until the birth of her first child in August.

The risk was that since she and Harvey had butted heads a few times in the past, she might find her job filled permanently instead of temporarily.

Maggie loved teaching, especially teaching math. But when to her amazement a publisher liked her proposal for a children's fun-filled math and puzzle book, and offered a contract on it dependent on her quick production of a finished manuscript, there was no way she could let the opportunity slip by. The problem was that not only did she have to produce a publishable book, but since it was a one-shot deal it certainly wouldn't make her independently wealthy and she would need her old job to return to. Would it be there for her?

There was no use, Maggie told herself, worrying over a decision she had already made and was acting on. She had taken her leave of absence, she had packed up and left Baltimore and soon she would be in Cedar Hill, New Hampshire, writing her book. The best thing she could do right now was to concentrate on her driving.

She realized, as she turned her focus back to the road and checked a few signs, that the miles had been flying by. She had driven through much of Massachusetts and would cross into New Hampshire before long. Then the mountains would be straight ahead. When she came to that part of the trip she could only hope that Dyna's directions for the final leg were correct. Dyna had many good points. Organization, however, was not one of them, as her mind tended to flit around many distracting thoughts.

Maggie remembered her first sight of her friend last summer on the tennis courts at the Highview resort in Maryland, and it made her smile. Dyna had been sitting yoga-style, meditating courtside in preparation for their simple, hotel-arranged, fun match. That and her following offbeat conversation had thrown Maggie for a while. Having spent much of her life around down-to-earth practicality, Maggie had been quite unprepared for someone like Dyna. It didn't take her long, though, to realize how totally likeable her new acquaintance was, despite or perhaps because of her oddness, and their friendship had endured beyond that vacation week. Their unexpected involvement and collaboration on a murder investigation during that vacation might also have had something to do with their lasting camaraderie.

Another thing that had endured from that week at the Highview was Maggie's relationship with Rob Clayton, the tennis pro there. They had met over a tennis lesson. Now, however, he would be giving tennis lessons to other women, many, many miles away from her. But she wasn't going to let herself worry about that either. They would be many miles apart, but the phone lines would keep them connected, calling each other, as they had promised, every night.

Lowell sped by, Manchester, Concord, and then less familiar names appeared on signs. Snow had begun to fall lightly, but the roads remained relatively clear. She finally turned off onto the two-lane highway Dyna had directed her to, keeping her fingers crossed that it was the right one, and before long billboards and motels were replaced by picturesque farm-houses and barns tucked against snowy hills. Maggie loved it.

She found the turn-offs onto smaller and smaller roads, some numbered, some named, that Dyna had written down for her and soon, to her excitement, she was pulling into Cedar Hill.

The small New England town sat postcard-pretty in the late afternoon sun, church steeples stretching high above white-shingled houses, a red brick school with flag flying in front, small shops, a bank, all interspersed with tall pines and red cedars.

Maggie's eyes flitted back and forth as she took it all in. To the right a mother pushed her rosy-cheeked baby in a stroller along the cleanly shoveled sidewalk, beside two-foot high piles of snow at the curb. Across the street on the left, people in parkas and ear-snuggling knitted caps walked or stood chatting in small, friendly-looking groups. Maggie soaked it up, her smile growing.

She came almost to the end of the main street, which to her delight was actually called Main Street, just as in all the "small town" movies she had ever seen, and took a sharp right onto Hadley Road. This, Dyna had promised, would take her to the Halls' cabin. Hadley, she found, narrowed quickly into a winding road that seemed to double back on the town, but, according to the map she had consulted, actually climbed a hill and slowly angled away from it. Maggie drove past dense woods on each side, once glimpsing a deer, or at least its white tail flashing as it leaped away.

Within a couple of minutes a small group of houses appeared, most seemingly vacant. Maggie checked their numbers and counted, finally stopping beside one whose driveway was the only one cleared of snow. The etched pine plaque hanging on a pole beside it said "Hall" and "Welcome." Maggie looked up at the house in amazement.

"I thought when they said cabin they meant cabin," she said aloud, realizing she had pictured a tiny log structure. The actual "cabin" was an A-frame house, wood-shingled, two-storied, and much larger than Maggie had expected. A blue

Ford rental car with a ski rack on its roof sat in the driveway next to a small detached garage. Dyna had already arrived. Maggie pulled her Chevy next to the Ford and turned off her ignition. The side door of the house leading to a small landing immediately flew open.

"Maggie! You're here!"

Dyna bounced down the few stairs, her thick, multi-shaded blond hair and long earrings flying out over her bulky sweatshirt, and hugged her friend as she climbed out of the car. "Was your trip okay? What do you think—isn't it great here? We *have* to go skiing—the weather's perfect. You *did* bring your ski clothes, didn't you?"

"Yes, Dyna," Maggie laughed, returning her friend's enthusiastic hug. "Yes to everything. Now, may I please bring my things into the house?" Maggie pulled open the back door of her car. Two bulging satchels tumbled out.

"I'll take these," Dyna said, grabbing them and jumping out of the way. Maggie reached in for her most precious cargo, the well-padded laptop computer. Taking one more box, she followed a still-chattering Dyna up the steps of the cabin.

"This is it," Dyna said, holding the side door open and waving Maggie through. She stepped into a small foyer that led immediately to a compact kitchen. Almond-colored appliances glistened in the sun that beamed through an octagonal side window. A raised counter and three stools divided the kitchen from the living area. Maggie headed for a round oak table beyond the counter and gently set her laptop on it.

She looked around at the rest of the living area, which contained a sofa and chairs upholstered in amber and blue tweed. A stone-faced fireplace was angled in the far corner opposite the sofa. Next to it a sliding glass door led to a redwood deck.

"This is terrific!" Maggie said.

Dyna beamed. "I knew you'd like it. C'mon up and see the bedrooms." She led Maggie up a winding, wrought-iron staircase. The master bedroom had a queen-sized bed, covered with a puffy yellow comforter, and its own bathroom. The smaller room held twin beds and pine furniture. A second bathroom opened off the hall.

"You take the bigger room, of course, 'cause you'll be here most of the time. The smaller one's always been mine anyway, and it has my initials scratched into the dresser to prove it. Hah! Do I remember Mom's reaction when she saw that! Are you going to leave your computer downstairs?"

Maggie nodded. "I loved that view of the woods through the sliding door, and I'll have more space to spread out my mess."

Dyna raised an eyebrow skeptically. "Little Miss Organized making a mess? I wonder what you call a mess—two papers not perfectly lined up with each other?"

"You'll see," Maggie said, laughing, "when you have to call for a dumpster to clear me out of here. Well, let's get the rest of my stuff."

When they brought in the final load and had kicked the door closed behind them, Dyna plopped onto the sofa. "What do you think about going into town tonight after dinner? Are you tired? There's a town meeting scheduled at the school. If we went you could meet just about everyone there in one swoop."

Maggie thought for a minute. She *was* tired from the long drive, but at the same time she was keyed up, excited to be here. She knew she couldn't just sit down and do nothing. Besides, a town meeting sounded so perfectly New-England-small-town. Her mind conjured up a gathering of several generations—grey-haired codgers, middle-aged and younger couples, some holding sleeping babies on their knees—sipping coffee and discussing who would organize the Fourth of July picnic, and should they cut down or try to save the old oak in front of the school.

"Would I need to dress up?" Maggie asked.

"No," Dyna flapped a hand. "I'll go like this."

Maggie looked at Dyna's Baltimore Ravens sweatshirt and faded blue jeans. "Okay, just let me hop in the shower."

"Wait, I'd better turn on the hot water first." Dyna went to the door opposite the side door in the foyer. "We turn the water heater off when the cabin's going to be empty," she explained. "Saves electricity. C'mon, I'll show you the whole thing, in case you need it when I'm gone."

Maggie peered over her shoulder as Dyna opened the metal cover of the circuit breaker box inside the utility closet. "This is the switch for the hot water," Dyna said, then pointed to the inside of the cover. "See, they're all marked on this diagram. And this is the main switch for the whole cabin. But you only need to know that if you want to re-wire switches or something. I don't suppose you're going to do that, are you?"

Maggie laughed. "No, I left my tools back in Baltimore."

Dyna closed the breaker box. "The water gets hot pretty quick. I picked up a frozen pizza. Should I put it in now? You'd have thirty minutes."

"That's all I need," Maggie called as she ran up the stairs and began pulling things out of her bags. By the time she stepped out of the shower she could smell the pizza baking, and her stomach gave a healthy growl. She dressed quickly, then struggled with her short brown hair, always a frustrating experience as the curls stubbornly resisted nearly every direction she tried to lead them, until Dyna called up the stairs that the pizza was ready.

Maggie looked at her reflection in the mirror and shrugged. "That'll do. I'm hungry." She put down her brush, stepped over a pile of clothing, and trotted down to dinner.

Night had fallen, which in New Hampshire in January meant the temperature had already dropped another ten to fifteen degrees by the time Maggie followed Dyna down the cabin's steps and climbed into the Ford parked in the driveway.

"Tonight I'll pull it into the garage," Dyna said. "Dad and Mom had the garage built after they bought the cabin. Sometimes it's a pain having to walk outside to get to it, but they couldn't attach it, and it's better than nothing. There's only room for one car, but I won't be here that long anyway." They had bundled up in parkas, boots, and gloves, and on hearing the wind whistling through the trees, grabbed hats on their way out the door. As Dyna backed down the driveway she said, "We could actually walk to town. It's close enough if you go through the woods." Then she added matter-of-factly, "Except we might freeze to death on the way back."

Maggie watched eagerly as they drove down Hadley to the turn, then rode along Main Street. Street lights glimmered on the snow and storefronts glowed, lit softly to show their wares. Dyna explained that since it was a Sunday night most shops were closed. Probably the best time for everyone to gather for a meeting, Maggie thought, images of what she considered a typical small town assembly still floating through her head. This was such a pretty, peaceful town. The perfect retreat for working on her project.

As Dyna turned down Washington Street to get to the school, however, all Maggie's cozy *It's a Wonderful Life* scenes splintered like a windshield hit with an icy snowball.

"Down with Warwick!" an angry group of people shouted, tramping in a circle and jabbing hand-drawn signs into the air with their thick-mittened hands.

"Keep Warwick out of Cedar Hill!" one burly man demanded, his glare aimed furiously at Maggie and Dyna as they drew near.

"Stop the rape of Cedar Hill!" a housewife screamed, leaning menacingly in their direction.

A small boy aimed a snowball in their direction, narrowly missing, and Maggie's eyes widened in surprise. What had she come to?

Chapter Two

"What's going on?" Maggie asked. She peered at the group milling about menacingly in front of the school.

"I don't know," admitted Dyna. She pulled the car into an empty space in the parking lot, and some of the marchers glared in their direction. "But whatever it is, I'll bet Regina White is at the head of it." Dyna seemed unconcerned, so Maggie climbed out of the car and followed her friend toward the building. "Uh-huh," Dyna said over her shoulder, "I was right. There she is. Hi, Regina!"

A thin, wiry woman dressed in a navy pea jacket and knitted cap from which a few wispy grey hairs escaped, looked over and squinted at them. Maggie saw that her face was lined, but full of energy and set with determination. She appeared to recognize Dyna and gave her a curt nod before turning back briskly to the matter at hand. That seemed to be keeping her small but loud group shouting and picketing. Whoever Warwick was, Maggie thought, he obviously wasn't on this group's A list.

An icy wind suddenly blew around the corner of the school. Maggie pulled her jacket collar closer and hurried with Dyna past the picketers. She helped Dyna tug open the heavy door to be greeted by welcoming warmth and an enticing aroma of coffee. They bustled in, dropped their jackets on a row of empty chairs next to the wall, and followed others gravitating to the refreshments table. Two dozen people milled about in

11

the combination gymnasium–meeting room, some beginning to take seats in the rows of chairs set up before a table and a podium. Two young women busily worked at laying out cookies and paper plates at opposite ends of the food table.

"Elizabeth! How you doing?" Dyna called out to one of them.

A slim, small-boned woman of about 25, with delicate features and a long, soft cloud of light brown hair looked up and smiled at Dyna.

"Liz, this is my friend Maggie Olenski. She's staying at our cabin for a few weeks. Maggie, Elizabeth Kerr runs the book shop on Main Street."

Elizabeth and Maggie smiled at each other and before Maggie had a chance to say anything Dyna asked, "What's going on out there?"

A tiny frown formed on Elizabeth's face. "The meeting tonight is to discuss changing the zoning law so that Jack Warwick can buy Big Bear Resort and turn it into a mining operation for granite. Some people are opposed to it, and Regina and her group are *very* opposed, for environmental reasons."

Dyna's mouth dropped open. "Sell Big Bear for mining? But it's such a great ski mountain." Maggie looked at Dyna's shocked face and feared for a moment she might run back out to join the picketers.

"Karin, does Alexander want to sell?" Dyna called to the other woman behind the table, making a hasty introduction to Maggie. Attractive, about thirty, with sleek, chin-length, dark brown hair and large brown eyes, Karin Dekens was married to one of the major owners of Big Bear, Dyna explained. Karin rearranged a couple of finger sandwiches before answering Dyna's question, then nodded. Maggie noticed her face had a studied neutrality.

"Alexander feels it would be a good idea to sell. The ski resort has been struggling financially for the last few years, and Alexander thinks this is our best option."

"But Paul loves the place. What about him? Does he want to sell?"

Karin looked at Dyna with her large eyes and said coolly, "Paul doesn't agree with Alexander."

At that point a tall, ruddy-cheeked man, whose blue ski sweater stretched over a paunchy middle, came up beside Karin and reached past her for a sandwich.

"These are for after the meeting," Karin said.

"But, dear one, you know I'm a growing boy." Alexander Dekens winked, patted his stomach, and grinned at Dyna. He acknowledged her introduction to Maggie, reached for a cookie, and sauntered away with another wink. Maggie noticed that Karin hadn't smiled at her husband's humor but had kept her eyes continuously on her work.

A tawny-haired young woman came up slowly and carefully to the table. She wore cream-colored stretch pants with a matching cream-colored cable knit sweater, and high-heeled, rust-colored suede boots. The outfit combined with her flowing hair was stunning and embellished her perfect figure. She spoke to Karin in a Southern accent, which surprised Maggie, who mentally tried to place it. Somewhere south of Maryland was all she could determine.

"Karin, I'm just parched. Could I please have a glass of punch?" She seemed to be having trouble with her balance, and reached a beautifully manicured hand out to the table to steady herself.

"Sure, Leslie." Karin introduced Leslie Warwick to Dyna and Maggie as she poured out the cold punch for her. Maggie realized that Elizabeth had suddenly disappeared.

"You picked quite a night to come meet the townspeople," Leslie said to Maggie. "I'd stay near the door to duck out fast if things start flyin'." She laughed, and walked unsteadily towards a chair in the front row. Maggie didn't think her heels were high enough to be the cause of her wobbling.

"Leslie's Jack Warwick's wife, of course," Karin explained after she had left. "Poor thing," she added, looking thoughtfully over Maggie's shoulder. "Excuse me, I'd better get some more ice for the punch."

Maggie followed Dyna over to two chairs near the center and sat down. There was some scuffling as others found seats, and just before the meeting was called to order Maggie noticed that Regina White and the picketers had quietly come in and seated themselves as a group in the back.

"That's the mayor, Tom Larson," Dyna whispered as a white-haired man in a grey cardigan sweater stepped up to the podium.

"Everyone find a seat?" he asked, looking around the room with a smile. He waited as the last of the talking quieted down. "Well, we have a pretty good turnout tonight. Since I'm sure you didn't show up to hear me talk about the town hall's new snow-blower, we'll get right down to the matter at hand. All of you probably know who Mr. Jack Warwick is." He indicated the navy-blue suited man seated at the front table. "Why don't we just let him say what he's got to say. Mr. Warwick?"

There was a smattering of applause, and Jack Warwick stepped up to the podium, nodding and smiling to the mayor and to the gathered townspeople. He was a man, Maggie judged, of about fifty, but a young, vibrant fifty. Average height with broad shoulders, Jack Warwick emanated an energy and magnetism that kept everyone's eyes glued to him, waiting for his first words. He leaned towards them, his ruggedly handsome face smiling under salt-and-pepper hair, and said, "Good people, I propose to save Cedar Hill."

"You propose to destroy it," a female voice said from the back, and Maggie wondered if it was Regina's. Warwick ignored the comment.

"I know your problems. I know your hardships. There have been fewer and fewer jobs. Young people are having to move away from their families, from the town they grew up in and love, to find means to support themselves." He paused, and Maggie saw a few heads nodding. "This town has depended greatly on tourists, skiers drawn to Big Bear Ski Resort. But as we all know, their numbers have decreased in the last few years because of the competition from newer, bigger resorts. This has hurt your economy, badly, to the point of death. I can save that economy by buying Big Bear and turning it into a thriving mining operation."

Warwick went on to enumerate the jobs that his company

would bring to the area, speaking glowingly of the changes—all positive—that would come to Cedar Hill. He ended with a promise to personally donate, once the contracts were signed, a substantial amount of money for renovation of the school as a symbol of his lasting interest in the town.

Maggie glanced around the room and realized that the building did need repairs. Some ceiling tiles hung loosely, there were signs of water damage, and the very chairs on which they sat looked to be on their last legs. What better way to win the parents over than to promise such enticements—a new and improved environment for their children?

"Mr. Warwick, I don't agree that your mining operation would be good for our town." Maggie looked over as a middle-aged woman, more elegantly dressed than most others there, stood to speak. "I own Ski Lady Boutique, an upscale women's salon featuring designer clothing. My business would not survive if Big Bear became a mining operation, nor would several others' businesses, such as Mr. Morgan's fine restaurant." She gestured to a man seated a couple rows behind her, and all heads, including Maggie's, turned to look. Mr. Morgan was a slim, dark haired man in his mid-thirties, who sat dourly with arms crossed tightly across his chest. To Maggie's surprise he did not rise to add his voice to the dress store owner's, but stayed silently in his seat.

Another man jumped up to voice his opinion in favor of the zoning change. He managed the supermarket in town, and he obviously knew an influx of new jobs and new people would be good for his business. Others rose to have their say—the manager of the ski shop against, the coffee shop owner for, and so on—and as far as Maggie could tell the townspeople were evenly divided.

Dyna pointed out Paul Dekens, Alexander's brother, who listened tensely but said nothing. Maggie saw that Paul was in much better shape than his older brother, looking as though he often used the ski slopes he cared about so much. A grim look marred his even features as he listened to the arguments, but Maggie saw his expression soften when Elizabeth caught his eye, as she moved near the refreshments table. Elizabeth, with her quiet ways, seemed to be distancing herself from the debate.

Suddenly Regina White jumped out of her seat in the back. "You talk of wanting to help this town!" she shouted. "I don't believe it for a minute. It's greed! You want all the money you can pull from that mountain." She waved her arm, vigorously jabbing it to the left, in the direction, Maggie assumed, of Big Bear. "You don't care about us. You don't care what you will do to the environment. It's all greed. Money in your pocket. And you think you'll get your way, because you have your friends in high places. You've greased a few palms. You say you want our approval, our vote. You just want us to keep quiet and not get in the way! Well, we won't. Listen to me, Cedar Hill, and vote 'No' to keep Warwick from destroying us!"

Jack Warwick tried to respond but she drowned him out, hurling more accusations, her voice rising with each one. Tom Larson stepped up, trying to calm things down, but Regina kept the floor, causing many uncomfortable looks and some angry ones. Finally two of her companions managed to pull her down to her seat.

One or two more people added their opinions, more quietly than Regina, then Mayor Larson brought the meeting to an uneasy end, saying that the town would vote on the issue in three weeks.

"I've got to run to the girls' room," Dyna said, popping up. "I'll be right back."

Maggie stayed in her seat and watched people as they moved around. She saw Alexander go up to Jack Warwick with an agreeable, eager-to-please look. He kept nodding and smiling as they spoke. His brother Paul scowled in their direction, but passed by and went over to talk to Elizabeth, who was now serving punch.

Leslie wobbled over to Jack and Alexander on her high-heeled boots and interrupted them, speaking in a too-loud voice. Her husband's face turned dark and he hissed something to her. Leslie colored, and she hissed something in return, then backed away, turning towards the refreshment table.

Maggie could hear Regina in the back, arguing with one of her picketers. He was urging her to leave with him, but she insisted she would stay, that she hadn't finished with Jack Warwick yet.

Dan Morgan, the restaurateur who had stayed silent during the public debate, stood talking to Karin Dekens. He looked a little less dour than he had during the meeting, and she smiled as she spoke, touching his arm. Her husband, Alexander, left Jack Warwick and passed near them. Maggie was surprised to see a bitter smirk turn up the corners of his mouth as he looked at them. Karin seemed aware of it, glancing up at him briefly, but ignored it and turned slightly away.

"Hello! You must be the writer who is moving into the Halls' place."

Maggie looked over with a start to see a plump, white-haired woman in an L.L. Bean skirt, blouse, and vest beaming at her. She introduced herself as Susan Larson, the mayor's wife. Maggie rose and shook her hand, pleasantly surprised to hear herself described as a writer.

"I'll be working on a book, but it's a math book, full of math games and puzzles for kids to play around with."

"Oh, math! How clever you must be. Numbers, I'm afraid, have always escaped me. I never could balance my own checkbook." Maggie smiled a polite smile, having heard that kind of comment many times before, particularly from women of Mrs. Larson's age group. She suspected it was more an attitude drummed into them from childhood than an actual math disability, and sometimes wished she could gather them all into some kind of remedial support group. A "You Really *Can* Do Math" group. Her own mother, who kept the books for the family bakery but still claimed she had no head for figures, would be her first member.

"I'm just so glad to be talking about something besides mountains and mining," Mrs. Larson said confidentially. "Since you're a newcomer, you won't have formed your opinion yet. I thought I'd better get to you before you started talking to others and choosing sides." The older woman's blue eyes twinkled, and she looked around with mock concern, as if one of Regina's picketers or Jack Warwick's supporters were likely to rush up and grab Maggie's ear any minute.

"A mayor's wife, and you don't like politics?" Maggie asked with a smile.

"Isn't that always the way?" Mrs. Larson laughed. "But Tom doesn't mind, and I don't expect him to join me at my Garden Club meetings. I hope you like our little town, as much as you've seen of it, that is?"

"I love it," Maggie enthused honestly, and Mrs. Larson's round face beamed. "Coming from a big city like Baltimore—"

A scream from the other side of the room turned her attention from Mrs. Larson to the group at the refreshments table.

Jack Warwick leaned heavily against the table. He clutched at his chest as he gasped for breath. His coffee mug still spun where it had landed on the floor.

"He's having a heart attack! Call an ambulance!" someone shouted.

"Oh my Lord!" Mrs. Larson said, and left Maggie as she rushed over to help. Maggie saw the mayor run to the wall phone, and several people helped Jack to the floor, loosening his tie and shirt, and generally doing what they could. Having no medical skills and no idea whatsoever of anything to do that would help, Maggie decided to stay back out of the way.

Dyna soon joined her, her eyes round with concern. "Wow, poor guy." She watched in silence for several moments, then couldn't help adding, "but I'll bet he smoked, and ate a lot of fatty foods." Maggie looked over at her health-conscious friend in surprise, but nodded, too overwhelmed for the moment to do anything else.

The ambulance arrived amid wailing sirens, and the townspeople watched the paramedics wheel Warwick out on the stretcher, an oxygen mask over his grey face and an IV line attached to his arm. Maggie silently wished him good luck, then looked around at the faces of the people she had just begun to know that night. They were universally solemn, many looking as stunned as she felt. But something was missing. It took her a moment to realize what it was.

She saw concern, but a distant concern, detached, the kind you would see on the faces of strangers watching a televised news report of an accident. But these were people who knew this man. One was even his wife. What Maggie realized she did not see was any sign of sorrow.

Chapter Three

The next morning, Maggie awoke in her puffy yellow bed and stretched. Bright sun shone through the window, telling her she had slept much later than her habitual 5:45 A.M. workday rising. Must remember to pull that shade at night, she thought with a smile, as she lifted her head enough to see the travel clock she had set up on the dresser. 9:05. A gust of wind blew snow from a nearby branch against the window panes, and Maggie snuggled deeper into the soft warmth of her flannel sheets and luxuriated in her leisure.

She had called Rob in Florida last night before turning in, and she wriggled contentedly as she reran some of the conversation through her head. Much of it had run in a highly intellectual vein:

"Miss you."

"Miss you more."

"Uh-uh."

"Uh-huh."

But Maggie had also shared her delight over Dyna's family "cabin," and the beauty of New Hampshire and Cedar Hill. Eventually she got around to the town meeting, giving him a condensed version of the debates and arguments and finishing with Jack Warwick's sudden illness. She had tried to sound as neutral as she could, but apparently he picked up on something in her voice that concerned him.

"I hope you can keep yourself out of the town's troubles,

20

Maggie," he had said. "You don't need the distraction. You're up there to work on your book."

"Oh, I know, I know. And I want to spend nearly every waking minute on it. The town will just have to solve its own problems without me," she had said, laughing.

Thinking of this now, though, Maggie squirmed. She was reminded of another phone conversation, this one with her brother Joe, telling her, *ordering* her to keep out of a murder investigation at her summer vacation. The perverse side of her had instantly resolved to ignore him. Which had gotten her into a pile of trouble.

Rob certainly wasn't ordering her to mind her own business, simply pointing out something with which she already agreed. Why then did she feel her interest in the town and its troubles immediately escalate? Did she unconsciously hope to some-how intervene in this zoning debate, to solve in some way their economic and environmental problems? Not likely. She was going to do only what she had come up here to do and nothing more. End of story.

Sounds of activity from the kitchen below broke into her thoughts. She flipped back the comforter with sudden energy and jumped out of bed, scrambling to locate her robe and slippers among her still unorganized clothing. Soon she trotted down the winding stairway to join Dyna.

"Hey, slugabed!" Dyna leaned over the garbage can as she deposited a cone of soggy coffee grounds and looked up. "I knew the smell of coffee would pull you down here." She looked unusually domestic, puttering behind the kitchen counter, mugs, plates, and spoons already pulled out of their cabinets and drawers. Maggie's eyes searched hopefully among the crockery for something edible to go with the cof-fee, but wasn't finding much. Then Dyna said the words she didn't want to hear.

"Hope you're not too hungry."

Maggie sighed. "No. Coffee's fine."

"We'll have to get to the store. I just picked up a few things in a hurry yesterday. How would you like your toast? Plain, or unadorned?"

Maggie grinned. "Can't beat unadorned. Here, let me take care of it. I think your tea water is ready." The microwave pinged and Dyna pulled out a glass measuring cup of hot water. She poured it over a greenish tea bag sitting in one of the mugs.

Maggie transferred two slices of toast from the toaster to the plates, then poured a mug of coffee for herself. She moved to the other side of the counter and climbed onto one of the stools.

"By the way," Dyna said as she seated herself on a second stool, "I forgot to tell you. I might get a job."

Maggie had just taken a bite of toast and she stopped in mid-chew to keep from choking. Dyna hadn't worked since her pet shop job last spring. Her inability to keep her thoughts to herself while waiting on a customer swathed in animal furs had pushed her into the ranks of the unemployed. Her previous employment had been in a paranormal bookshop whose otherworldly connections could not keep it from going bankrupt. And before that, well, the truth was that Dyna didn't *have* to work. A generous trust fund set up by her grandmother kept her in herbal teas, and she worked only to please her industrious parents and possibly to fill her time.

"What kind of a job?" Maggie asked, having safely swallowed.

"Well, there's this health food store back in Baltimore, near the Inner Harbor. They advertised for help and I went over. Pretty neat place. I think I'd like it there. The store has a nice feel, you know, a good aura. But I didn't give them a final answer 'cause I wanted to come up here, get you settled in and all."

Ah, health food. Maggie had noticed Dyna's interest in healthy eating gradually increase to the point that now she was almost totally vegetarian and avoided caffeine and alcohol. The pizza she had picked up for last night's dinner had been meatless.

"That sounds like a great situation for you. I hope you don't lose it, though, because of me."

"Oh, no. I'm pretty sure they'll hold it for me. I just haven't, you know, made up my mind totally." She pulled her tea bag out of her mug and dropped it into the sink.

Maggie stirred her coffee, her mind picturing Dyna ringing up sales of soy milk and salt-free sweet potato chips. It seemed right to her. At least, she thought, Dyna wouldn't be at risk of getting into arguments with the clientele. Presumably any opinions she offered there would just be preaching to the choir.

"So, you talk to Rob lately?" Dyna asked.

"Last night. He's pretty busy, getting the tennis camp started and all. They got a good turnout."

"Guess your mom's not too sad he's down in Florida, huh?"

Maggie sighed. "Probably not. You know, she's not saying much, but she's obviously cool with the whole idea of Rob and me as a couple."

"So she's never said exactly what she has against him?"

"No, but I can guess. Probably something like he's not from Baltimore and she hasn't known his family since the day he was born, and all his neighbors, teachers, et cetera, et cetera."

"But that's so weird. I mean, nobody knows anybody that well anymore. People move around so much."

"My folks don't. And none of their friends do, except to the beach for two weeks in the summer. The same beach, and usually the same beach house." Maggie took another bite of her unadorned toast. "When Mom got engaged to Dad, they had known each other since high school and their fathers had even worked together. But when they went to the church office to arrange the wedding, the secretary there, an old woman who knew Mom's family and had been running the office since before typewriters were invented probably, looked at her and said, 'You couldn't find someone from your own parish?' "

"Wow. That verges on inbreeding."

Maggie laughed. "Well, that's where she's coming from, so I'm not expecting miracles."

"Sounds like she'd even be suspicious of a miracle, considering, you know, it would have to come from outside the neighborhood."

"Speaking of miracles, I wonder how Jack Warwick is doing."

Dyna looked up. "Yeah, me too. He didn't look too good when they took him away. And the hospital is at least fifteen miles away. It's a good one, though." Dyna looked thoughtful for a while, then a tiny smile appeared. "It's funny, you know, what some people think to do when a crisis like that comes up." She crossed her legs.

"I was with Annette Raison just before it happened. She was in charge of all the food last night and things were going okay so we got to talking. Well, when Warwick got sick and staggered back against the food table, you know what Annette did? Not rush over to *him* like most people did. She ran to the punch bowl and held onto it for dear life so it wouldn't be knocked off."

Maggie smiled. "We all have our priorities, I guess. There are probably some good EMTs who would make terrible food handlers." And I would be awful at both, she admitted to herself. She vowed privately to sign up for a CPR course the next time she saw one advertised back home. She didn't like that feeling of helplessness she'd had last night as others stepped in to aid Jack. There wouldn't always be someone else around to take over. What if an emergency happened in her classroom?

She also knew she should work at upgrading her cooking from the hurry-up, just-add-water-and-heat level. And she would. Some day.

Maggie finished her not-so-hearty breakfast as Dyna talked about the various slopes on Big Bear and which ones were best to start out on, then trotted up the stairs to get herself ready for her first full day in Cedar Hill.

Maggie followed Dyna out of the small supermarket on Main Street, carrying half of their fully packed brown grocery bags. Maggie rested hers on the hood of the blue Ford while Dyna pulled off one of her thick gloves to fit the key in the trunk.

"I still can't believe they don't carry tofu," Dyna complained. "I mean, it's practically a staple nowadays, isn't it?"

Not in my refrigerator, Maggie thought, but murmured something noncommittal. She hoisted her bags over to the open trunk and dropped them in. "At least they did have Chunky Monkey," she said, looking with satisfaction at the half gallon of her favorite decadent ice cream nestled near the top of one of her bags. Break-time from her writing, she thought, was going to be delicious.

"Well, hellooo!"

Maggie looked up over the trunk lid and saw a fortyish, apple-shaped woman in snug pants and waist-length red jacket coming down the street towards them. Her small, dark eyes—like apple seeds, Maggie thought—darted around alertly, apparently unwilling to miss a thing as she closed in on the new girl in town.

"That's Annette, the punch bowl savior I told you about," Dyna muttered.

Maggie nodded, stifling a laugh, and closed the trunk. She stepped up onto the curb with Dyna.

"I don't suppose you girls have heard." Annette said, barely acknowledging Dyna's introduction to Maggie, her voice solemn but her face lit with excitement.

"About what?" Dyna asked.

She kept them waiting as she drew a dramatic breath. "Jack Warwick is dead. And not from a heart attack. They suspect poison!"

"Oh my gosh!" Dyna cried.

Maggie said, "Oh, no," softly to herself.

Annette folded her hands over her middle, a satisfied look on her face, clearly savoring the moment.

"The sheriff and his men collected all the leftover food from the meeting late last night," she said. "We had stored it in the school refrigerator. There was quite a bit left, of course, since no one stayed around much after the ambulance left. But I told him," she said, jutting her chin up, "it couldn't possibly be from any of our food. After all, I made most of it myself!"

"Lots of people ate the same things last night. Nobody else got sick, did they?" Maggie asked.

"Of course not. Which only goes to show," Annette said, nodding her head firmly. "Well, I'll let you girls be on your way." She began glancing around, obviously searching for someone else to spread the dreadful, exciting news to. "Terrible thing to happen in our town," she said as she turned away towards the supermarket, certain to find new quarry there. "Poor Mrs. Warwick," she said and added, almost as an afterthought, "and poor Elizabeth."

Elizabeth? Why would Annette feel sympathy for the young bookstore manager? Maggie barely had time to register that thought when Annette turned back and called, "Oh, by the way. The sheriff will probably be calling on you sometime today. He's questioning everyone who was at the meeting last night."

At this Maggie groaned. She slumped against the car and looked at Dyna.

"What?" Dyna asked, her face a picture of innocence. "Don't blame me. I didn't do it."

The sheriff didn't waste any time. As they drove up the winding road and approached the cabin Maggie saw his car pulling into their driveway. Dyna pulled in next to him and jumped out as soon as she turned off the ignition. She called excitedly to the uniformed man who had climbed out of his own car.

"Hey, John! How you doing? You're the sheriff now? I can't believe it! Last I saw you, you were still a deputy."

The tall, gangly sheriff turned to Dyna and looked at her with an easy smile. "Last I saw you, you were going to witching school. Got your diploma yet?" Maggie's lips twitched as she remembered Dyna's tale about her one-time dreams of learning "good" witchcraft, and about the school that actually taught it somewhere in New Hampshire.

Dyna shrugged and sighed. "No, that just didn't work out. One of life's disappointments, you know?"

Sheriff John kept a very straight face as he nodded. When

he looked over at Maggie, though, she saw a smile in his eyes. "You must be Miss Olenski. John Severin." He held out a large hand, and Maggie shook it, feeling his strength and confidence in it. She invited him into the cabin, and he helped them carry in their bags, crunching over the packed snow with large black boots. Dyna unpacked and stowed away the groceries while Maggie fixed a fresh pot of coffee and pulled out mugs.

"So you're investigating Jack Warwick's death, huh?" Dyna asked John as she joined them in the living room with her mug of herbal tea. She sat on the couch, curling her feet under her, a look of wonder on her face. She was apparently still getting used to his new status. "Did you find something in the food?"

"No, not yet. But it'll take a while for all the testing. My guess is that what killed Jack Warwick was in his coffee cup, and in his cup only." John took a long, trusting drink from his own cup, then asked if either of them had seen or heard anything suspicious last night.

Maggie thought back carefully, remembering various small, interesting things she had seen, but nothing she would actually call suspicious. "When Jack got sick, I had my back to him, talking to the mayor's wife, Mrs. Larson. I'm afraid I wasn't aware of anything to do with Jack until someone screamed."

"Me neither," Dyan agreed. "I was talking—no, listening— to Annette Raison. You know how she goes on sometimes. But she always seems to know everything that's happening. You should talk to her."

"We already have," John said, a rueful smile on his face. "It seems she was too busy handling the refreshments and talking to you to see anything out of line." He sighed. "That's probably about what we'll hear from everyone there, but we still have to check it out. Nobody notices something that they're not expecting to see, it seems. This may be a long investigation."

Dyna's eyes lit up. "Maybe Maggie can help you."

"Dyna!"

"But you're good at that," Dyna protested, ignoring the look

Maggie was sending her. "We pretty much met last summer over a dead body, which is a long story I'll have to tell you sometime. But it's mainly because of Maggie that the murderer's in prison now," she explained to John. "I'll bet she would be a big help."

John took a deep breath, his eyebrows wriggling in consternation. Maggie hurried to end his uncomfortable struggle between duty and tact. "Don't worry. I came up here to work on a math book, not become Maggie Olenski, Private Investigator."

John let out some of his breath, nodding. "Murder investigation is a serious thing." He looked over at Dyna. "And sometimes a dangerous thing. Best leave it to the people who know what they're doing."

"But—" Dyna started to object.

"John's right," Maggie said, although the implication that she wouldn't know what she was doing rankled just a bit. "I have every faith in John's competence. Don't you?"

Dyna could hardly say she didn't trust her old friend's ability, so she was effectively silenced, reduced to a somewhat reluctant nod. Maggie quickly changed the subject, inviting John to join them for lunch.

"No, thank you," he said, draining his mug and setting it down. "Best I get a move on. Time to start proving my competence."

Maggie saw the same smile in his eyes as he rose that she had noticed earlier. She walked him to the door, where he thanked them both for their time. "If you think of anything we should know, please call," he said, then tramped down the snowy stairs.

"I still think we could help," Dyna complained, when Maggie closed the door. "Don't you? Aren't you curious?"

"It's not my business, and besides, I don't have time. I have a deadline to meet. And I thought you were going back soon to take that health food job."

"I'll go back, but not this instant. Unless you want me to, of course. I just thought, you know, I'd be up here for at least a couple more days. To, you know, show you around. We haven't even gone skiing yet!"

Dyna looked at her with such a sad puppy look, Maggie had to laugh. "I don't want you to go this instant. And I'd love to ski. But really, nothing else. Dyna, I've got to . . ."

"Write the book. I know, and I won't keep you from it, I promise. Except today. You're still settling in. And look at that sun shining out there. We can't waste that. It's a perfect day to hit the slopes. Right?"

Maggie didn't have to look to agree. It was a beautiful day, and she did want to go out with Dyna while she was here. Since Dyna had gone to so much trouble just to help Maggie get situated here, she really felt she owed her at least an afternoon together. But as she loaded Mrs. Hall's skis onto the Ford's ski rack after their quick lunch, dressed now in her ski pants, jacket, and a couple of layers of shirts and sweaters, she wondered guiltily, and a little worriedly, if she were becoming a procrastinating writer already. Before she had even begun.

Chapter Four

"Well, this is it. What do you think?" Dyna asked as she steered her car into a parking space.

Maggie looked up at the slopes of Big Bear. Skiers, looking like butterflies in their neon-colored clothing, zigzagged through the snow high above. Bright sun sparkled off the chairlifts as they glided up the mountain, picking up and dropping off ticketholders at each end like a lazy assembly line.

She climbed out of the car and took a deep breath of the cold, clear air. "Wonderful! I can't wait to get up there!"

First, however, came the job of lugging their equipment to the lodge, the part of skiing Maggie liked the least. She often wished ski resorts, like hotels, would provide bellhops to run up to your car and manage all your bulky, heavy things for you. Or at least luggage carts. She assumed it was a kind of test. If you couldn't carry your equipment, then you weren't worthy of being a skier and shouldn't be there in the first place.

Maggie joined Dyna in pulling boots out of the trunk and skis and poles off the rack on the car roof. They snapped everything into the proper carriers and trudged off toward the lodge, Maggie trying to stop thinking of herself as a pack mule in Thinsulate. When they came to the entrance they paused, catching their breath, and Maggie looked up at a huge grizzly bear posed in the standing attack position, its teeth bared high above her head.

"Wow!"

"He's the Big Bear mascot," Dyna explained. "And don't worry, he was never real. Plastic and acrylic and stuff like that. I heard Regina was getting all geared up to protest animal cruelty when he was first set up—designing posters, organizing a demonstration—until someone finally clued her in."

Maggie smiled. "She seems to have a protesting personality."

"You got that right," Dyna said. "Although, if it had been a real bear, I would have been right with her. If I'd been here, of course." She pointed to the left. "That's where we get our tickets."

Maggie tramped over with Dyna to the ticket window and leaned her skis against one of several high wooden racks next to it. She bought her ticket, attached it to a D-ring on her jacket, then picked up her ski boots and followed Dyna into the lodge.

"The food and stuff is up here. The lockers are downstairs," Dyna explained. "We can leave our snow boots there, and I think I'm going to take off one of these sweaters and stow it. It's so sunny and calm today I was getting too warm just walking from the car."

"So was I," Maggie said. She had unzipped her jacket the moment she stepped inside. The aroma of grilled hamburgers and coffee drew her attention as she walked past the dining area on her right. Her gaze swept over a large room with an open-beamed ceiling and a cafeteria set up at the far end. A small fire glowed in a centrally placed circular fireplace surrounded by benches. A few people lounged with their feet propped up close to it, sipping from glass mugs, looking lazily contented. Large windows gave spectacular views of the slopes.

Maggie's pace had slowed, taking all this in, and she would have stopped altogether if she hadn't glimpsed Dyna disappearing around a corner. Maggie hurried to catch up after her. The lower level had vending machines, benches, and the lockers Dyna had promised.

They chose an empty bench and sat down to change from

their snow boots to the shin-high ski boots, adding a second layer of thick socks. Other skiers milled around, some heading for the restrooms, others dropping coins into the vending machines, most moving clumsily and noisily in the heavy boots designed for safety and maneuverability on the slopes, but not for easy walking.

As Maggie was stowing her unneeded gear in a small locker, she heard Jack Warwick's name mentioned. She glanced around and saw two young men wearing matching red jackets with white crosses on the sleeves—ski patrollers. They sat a few benches away, holding Styrofoam cups of coffee and apparently discussing the incident of last night. But Maggie couldn't say for sure with half their words disappearing into the din. Without a second thought she closed up her locker and moved to the bench opposite them, sitting down at the end. She began fiddling with her boots, bent nearly double, her ears perked in their direction.

"I'm sorry the old guy popped off and all," the dark-haired one said, "but at least that'll stop the sale of Big Bear."

His blond companion nodded.

"Paul was so mad about the whole thing, though, I mean the sale idea," the darker one added, half grinning, "that I almost wonder if he did it, you know, slipped something into the old guy's drink. A lot of his problems sure got solved."

"Keep your mouth shut," the blond ski patroller said, flushing. He glanced around the room with a scowl and Maggie, who had chanced a peek in their direction, immediately looked down. "C'mon," he said, standing up and dumping his cup into a trash can. "Let's get out of here." They stomped off, and as they disappeared around the corner Maggie straightened up, realizing that Dyna was now nearby and had likely heard them too. Dyna raised an eyebrow at Maggie but said nothing, only handing Maggie the gloves and hat she had left near the locker. They both headed for the stairs.

I was just curious, Maggie insisted to herself, mentally arguing her non-involvement in the town's mystery as she climbed upwards. Suddenly she got a faceful of Dyna's jacket as Dyna abruptly stopped near the top. Paul Dekens had rounded the corner in a hurry and nearly collided with her.

"Whoops, excuse me" he said, stepping back out of the way. He was dressed in stretch ski pants and turtleneck, but holding a thick file of papers. "Back in town, huh?" he said to Dyna. "Are your folks here too?"

"No, I'm just here for a couple days getting my friend Maggie, here, settled. She'll be staying at our place for a while."

"Great," he said, turning to Maggie. "I saw you at the meeting last night. You picked a heck of a time to come, I'm afraid."

"It wasn't exactly what I expected."

Paul nodded. Maggie thought he looked distracted, but much less tense than he had the night before.

He asked Dyna, "Did you see Elizabeth today? This might be hard on her, the police talking to her and all. Her mother died just a few months ago, you know—her heart, finally—and Elizabeth's still getting over it. She doesn't need any more stress."

"No, we haven't seen her since last night. But we could stop in at the bookstore on the way back home and see how she's doing."

Paul smiled, and Maggie was struck with how much more attractive he was without the grim look he had worn last night. She guessed his age at early thirties, young for someone in his position. "That'd be great. Maybe—"

He was interrupted by a call from a Big Bear employee at the bottom of the stairs. After a quick, "Nice meeting you," to Maggie he trotted down the stairs and disappeared from sight.

As they retrieved their skis outside and headed for the nearest lift, Dyna said, "Paul's a great guy, really. Don't pay attention to that remark we heard downstairs."

"Remark?" Maggie asked vaguely, then looked ahead past Dyna. "Is that a good slope to start on? The lift line is nice and short right now. I need to limber up first on an easy one and get my balance." She chattered on while stepping into her skis and moving over to the line, not sure if she was trying

to convince Dyna or herself, that, despite appearances downstairs at the lodge, she was not getting interested in the mystery of Jack Warwick's murder.

The chair lift on the beginner's slope moved slowly, and
Maggie enjoyed the ride, soaking up the view, feeling the
combination of cold air and warm sun on her face. But on her
exit from the chair at the top she wobbled uncertainly, while
Dyna slid smoothly over to the edge of the hill.

"Your mom's skis are a little longer than mine," Maggie
said, catching up to Dyna. "But that's okay. I've been putting
off getting this size, but now I'll get used to them and won't
want to go back to my own. Maybe I should say *if* I get used
to them."

"You will. You're just a little shaky 'cause it's your first
time out. I've skied a couple weekends in Pennsylvania already this year. The snow's much better here, though. See you
at the bottom."

Maggie watched Dyna push off and whoosh her way down
like a pro. She, however, began her descent more cautiously
and was happy to stay upright all the way down, making her
turns careful and wide.

They rode the lift again, and her second run was better. She
felt her confidence return along with her balance. Her turns
became tighter, and she let her speed pick up.

"You're doing great," Dyna said. "Ready for an intermediate slope yet?"

"Almost. Do you mind one more run here?"

"Fine with me." Dyna skated over to the short line at the
lift, Maggie close behind, and soon they were scooped up by
the double chair, pulling the safety bar down as they began
their ascent. As they rode up on the gently swinging chair,
Maggie watched the skiers below, mostly beginners and children, all somewhat anonymous-looking with the camouflage
of ski hats and goggles.

Maggie's attention was caught by a young mother with her
child as she skied down the hill with him, his small skis inside
the "V" of her own, she lightly holding his shoulders, guiding

him in long, wide, slow turns. He looked almost ready to be on his own.

"Hey, I think that's Karin Dekens," Dyna cried. "You know, Alexander's wife. I recognize that green-and-white outfit. My gosh, that must be Ethan. I can't believe it! He's gotten so big!"

Maggie looked at them, taking in Karin's tender solicitousness and motherly pride. They watched until the lift took them out of view.

"Ethan must be about four now," Dyna said. "He's named after his great-grandfather, Alexander's and Paul's grandfather, who started up this resort back in the thirties or forties. I heard he began with just one rope tow that pulled skiers up the hill. Can you imagine? He must have had a lot of guts and determination."

"Mmm. From what I've seen so far, he might have passed on some of that determination to Paul, but not very much to Alexander. By the way, I thought I noticed a certain coolness between Karin and Alexander last night," Maggie said.

"Yeah, I wouldn't be surprised. From what I hear, Alexander's gambling's been getting worse. Annette told me last night that she thinks he's got into a lot of debt because of it, which is why he's so anxious to sell the resort—to raise cash. He never cared about the resort that much. She says it all must be rough on Karin, who loves it here, for herself and for Ethan.

"Paul, of course, does too," Dyna went on. "He wants to continue his grandfather's work, to build on it. Unfortunately, he's only one stockholder. Some cousins own parts of it too, and from what Annette says they live far away and care only about profits and losses."

"You know that gives Paul a strong motive to murder Jack Warwick," Maggie said. "Killing him, I assume, stops the negotiations, and Paul keeps his ski resort."

"I know," Dyna said reluctantly, her face wrinkling with concern. "But I know Paul just couldn't do something like that. He just couldn't."

"Maybe you're right. But that motive will keep him high

on the suspect list, I'm afraid, unless they find someone to replace him."

Maggie suddenly realized their chair was nearly at the top of the slope. She focused her attention on positioning her skis and poles properly to disembark, and, unlike her first attempt, skied off and away from the chair smoothly.

As she and Dyna adjusted gloves and poles, preparing to push off once more from the top, Maggie said, "I saw the way Paul was looking at Elizabeth last night. That, and his asking about her with such concern today, tells me he has strong feelings for her."

Dyna looked at Maggie, her face clearly showing this was a new idea to her. "You might be right. I wonder if Elizabeth is aware of it, though. She seems kinda down, maybe because of her mother and all. I don't think she's been in much of a mood for seeing anyone."

"What about that comment Annette made this morning? She seemed to be hinting that Elizabeth would be upset about Jack Warwick's death."

"Yeah, that was pretty weird. I don't know what she meant, but Annette's a big gossip, as you probably noticed. Half the time I think she's just trying to stir something up."

Maggie nodded, but she still wondered. She and Dyna pushed off together, Maggie keeping up with Dyna easily now. She skied on auto-pilot, though, her mind flashing over Paul, Alexander, Karin, and Elizabeth. Suddenly she realized what she was doing and braked in the middle of a turn.

Stop this, Maggie! You told Dyna you weren't going to go looking for things, and there you were, at the drop of a hat, eavesdropping on those ski patrollers back at the lodge. Now you're trying to come up with suspects. Remember what you're here for. To write a math book. Nothing else!

"Anything wrong?" Dyna called to her from the base of the slope.

"No," Maggie called back, annoyed with herself. She dug her poles in and aimed her skis downward again. Yes. Too much was wrong, but it wasn't up to her to make it right.

"On your right," a voice behind her called, and a skier

swooshed by, passing a few feet to her right side. Maggie watched as he made it speedily to the bottom, then followed at her own, slower pace. She came to a stop a few feet from Dyna and pointed one pole in the direction of the intermediate slopes.

"Let's move on over. I'm ready for something that will make me work harder and think less."

"Great!" Dyna turned and led the way to the next chairlift some distance away. Maggie followed, pushing with her poles, skating on the flat terrain. It took much more effort than skiing downhill, but she was grateful for it, hopeful that it would help clear her head of things she didn't want there.

However, as they passed in line with one of the lodge windows, she glanced over and caught sight of Karin Dekens inside, lit up by the sharply angled beams of the winter sun. Karin still wore her green-and-white jacket, but her hat and goggles had been removed. She faced a man whose back was to the window. It might have been her husband, Alexander; Maggie couldn't tell, but he was obviously upset about something, his hands chopping at the air as he spoke.

What's going on, Maggie immediately wondered, then quickly forced herself to look away, up the slope. She clamped her jaw and silently repeated a mantra as she kept moving. In time to each forward push of a ski the words sounded in her head: "I won't get into it. I won't get into it. I won't get into it!"

They skied the rest of the afternoon, trying out one slope after another, Maggie pushing herself hard. During resting time, if her thoughts strayed back to Jack Warwick and the problems he had generated she quickly moved her mathematician's mind to calculating the angles of slopes and the rate of speed and distance covered by the skiers. There weren't too many other skiers, though, which surprised her on this perfect ski day, and she mentioned it to Dyna.

"Big Bear's been getting battered by competition from some of the newer, bigger resorts," Dyna said. "They have more money to advertise and to offer special deals. It's a shame, because a lot of people don't know what they're missing. This might be a small place, but it's still got a lot to offer. I love it here."

At the bottom of one of the harder runs, after four hours of skiing, Maggie looked at Dyna's red cheeks and nose and grinned, sure that hers were the same.

"Had enough?" she asked.

Dyna nodded. "Uh-huh."

They headed back to the lodge and wearily racked up their skis. There was no sign of Paul Dekens, or of Karin and Ethan as they walked into the dining area, shaking snow out of their hair and rubbing their cold hands. Dyna suggested they stop and get mugs of hot mulled cider and relax a while by the crackling fire, a suggestion that didn't take much coaxing with Maggie.

Deep shadows now covered the mountain, and a wind had picked up, sending puffs of powdery snow into the trees. Maggie shivered as she watched it through the large windows, and leaned a little closer to the fire, happy now to be comfortably indoors. Most of the other skiers had left or were leaving, although she noticed a few adventurous ones arriving, getting set for a few hours of night skiing.

She sipped her warm, spicy drink and stretched her legs out lazily onto the low hearth. She felt she could stay right there forever.

Eventually, though, her stomach growled and she looked over at Dyna. Dyna looked as enervated as she felt.

"I guess we should go home and fix dinner."

"Uh-huh."

"We bought all that food this morning."

"Uh-huh."

"Did we get anything that says 'Add water and heat?' "

"I sure hope so."

Neither moved, and they stayed where they were until all the light had disappeared outside except for the slope lights now dotting the view. Finally Maggie stirred, thinking of the trek back to the car they still faced, loaded up with all their equipment. Better do it while they still had an ounce of energy left. She pulled a reluctant Dyna to her feet and aimed her towards the lodge door. There they paused to zip, reglove, and brace themselves for the icy blast sure to be waiting on the other side.

After a dinner that filled them up with a minimal amount of effort, Maggie felt her energy slowly revive. She lingered for a while on the counter stool, sipping coffee, letting the caffeine do its work. When she found her thoughts toying with ways to present math puzzles she knew she was ready. She helped Dyna clean up, then went to the oak table to turn on her computer, eager to finally begin the work she had come all the way up here to do. She sorted through her notes, and began spreading papers around her.

"I can practice my yoga upstairs, and let you work in peace," Dyna said, folding up a dish towel and hanging it over the oven door handle. "I've been working on Sirshasan—you know, the headstand—and haven't quite got it yet. But I'm okay on Padmasan." At Maggie's questioning look she explained that was the lotus position. "I've got that down pat, no problem there. But I'm still having some trouble with Soorya Namaskas. That's where you bend over, touch your knees with your head and put your hands flat on the floor. I can get fingertips there, but not the rest yet."

"Well, good luck," was all Maggie could think of to say. Dyna had many interests, and for as long as they lasted, she threw herself into them wholeheartedly. Maggie wondered how long the yoga would last. She watched Dyna trip up the winding wrought-iron stairs and disappear into her room. She turned her attention to her laptop and stared at the blank screen for several moments, trying to organize her thoughts.

Thoughts of murder and motives tried to creep in, and she pushed them away firmly to focus on math puzzles. Still, nothing was appearing on her monitor. Well, might as well type in the title page. Perhaps that would get her juices flowing. She typed in "Fun with Math," looked at it and erased it, replacing it with "Math Games and Puzzles." Better? Maybe "Math Can Be Fun?" No. She went back to "Math Games and

Puzzles," typed her own name underneath it, and decided to print it out to see how it looked. She could hang it on the wall beside her for inspiration.

A tiny light at the base of her key pad blinked. Oops, battery's running low. Should have hooked up the power adapter. Where is it? Maggie looked around, then realized she didn't remember unpacking the thing. She must have brought it, though. Didn't she?

She stood up and went through a couple of boxes on the floor. No power adapter. Her suitcase? No, she had unpacked that thoroughly and knew it hadn't been there. Shoot! She hadn't brought it!

Maggie looked back at the screen. A warning sign had popped up. Her laptop would be useless in about two minutes, and would remain so until she could get hold of a power adapter. She sank into her chair and ran her hands through her hair in frustration.

Her evening was now shot, and instead of spending the whole day tomorrow as she had intended, inside, working hard, she'd have to go out shopping. Who knew if there was even a store in Cedar Hill that carried computer stuff? She might have to go searching from town to town for one. And with her luck she'd probably stumble over another dead body on the way!

"Aaarrrggghhhh." Dyna's groan floated from her room as her body stretched for some yoga move.

"My feelings exactly!" Maggie called back. "Double!"

Chapter Five

Maggie pulled on her boots and looked around the small foyer of the cabin for her hat.

"You're sure you don't mind if I go out to Big Bear without you?" Dyna asked, for probably the fourth time that morning. They had risen early and fixed a sumptuous breakfast of poached eggs with hollandaise sauce over English muffins. While washing up, Dyna noticed that a gentle snow had begun to fall and declared how it was her most favorite of all conditions in which to ski.

"No, honestly, Dyna. I want you to go," Maggie said. Besides, she knew sending Dyna off to the slopes would leave her with that much more quiet time at the cabin. Maggie saw her hat hiding on the floor behind Dyna's boots. She grabbed it and pulled it on.

"At least I could drive you there, couldn't I?" Dyna said, looking torn. "I don't want you to get lost."

"Don't worry, I had a sashful of badges in Girl Scouts. And these are my most favorite of all conditions for taking a walk through the woods. See you later."

Maggie pulled open the side door and trotted down the steps before Dyna could say anything more.

At the end of the driveway Maggie turned left to hike the few yards down the road to the footpath that wound through the woods. Dyna had pointed it out as they drove past it yesterday afternoon, explaining that it was a short cut to Main

Street. She could have taken her own car, but Maggie felt a need to work off some frustrated energy still with her from last night after her laptop went dead.

When she stepped into the woods Maggie was immediately enveloped in the perfect silence of tall trees and softly falling snow, and she felt her tension fade. Snowmobilers had packed down the snow so that the path was walkable, but happily there was no sign of them now. It was so quiet she could almost hear the flakes land, and she was transported to another world.

After walking a while, since she was all alone, she tilted up her head and stuck out her tongue to catch a few flakes. They were cold and delicious, just as they had been when she was ten years old. Although she had said it lightly, Maggie realized what she said was true. These conditions *were* her favorite for taking walks.

She noticed no signs of any wildlife as she went along— no squirrels, chipmunks, or birds twittering around, which caused her to picture small creatures peeking out from their cozy nooks, shaking their heads in amazement at this foolish, two-legged creature, outside in the cold and damp instead of sensibly tucked away like them. She grinned. A little snowfall certainly seemed to bring out the child in her. Before long she'd find herself plopped on her back making snow angels as she had loved to do in kindergarten.

Maggie grabbed a long stick lying in her way and carried it with her as she walked. She tried swinging it as a tennis racquet, remembering the lesson Rob had given her last summer on her backhand, but decided the slim branch made a better golf club or hockey stick and batted at a pinecone or two. She walked on in this manner, enjoying her isolated world until the path took her over a small rise and back into civilization.

She stepped out onto the sidewalk of Main Street, and shook her mind back to the real world. Time to get down to business. She remembered Dyna's directions to the shop she thought was most likely to carry a power adapter and turned left, picking up her pace, not sure how far to go but taking the opportunity to check out a little more of the Cedar Hill shopping area close up. With the predominance of huge malls back in Baltimore, where you left your car in a multi-level garage, Maggie was still getting used to the novelty of stores that people could actually walk to or park in front of.

A horn beeped, and she turned to see the mayor's wife, Susan Larson, drive by, waving. She waved back, smiling, and found herself thinking how really nice this little town was, in so many ways. If only people didn't happen to get murdered here.

Maggie looked into the windows of a gift shop as she walked by, passed a small bakery, a dress shop, and a pharmacy, and eventually came to the office supply store Dyna had directed her to. A large CLOSED sign hung at the door. Her stomach dropped, and she stood frozen to the spot, staring at the dreadful sign. Now what?

Maggie could have kicked herself for not calling first, for not having at least made a back-up plan. She looked around helplessly, and her gaze fell on the shop across the street. "The Book Nook." Quite possibly the book shop Elizabeth managed.

Maggie remembered Paul Dekens' request that they check on Elizabeth, and Dyna's offer to stop in on her yesterday, both forgotten in their après ski lethargy. Why not do it now, she thought, and possibly get directions to another computer place at the same time? She climbed over the snow bank at the side of the road and crossed the street.

The bell over the door tinkled lightly when Maggie walked in, and Elizabeth looked up from the rear of the small shop and smiled. She stood at a table of books, clipboard in hand, wearing a soft-looking peach-colored sweater and brown skirt that complemented her coloring. Her light brown hair curled gently onto her shoulders.

"You're Dyna's friend Maggie, aren't you? Welcome to my little shop," she said.

"Thank you. I was so glad to see you open this early," Maggie said. She loosened her jacket, suddenly shivering as a few snowflakes slid from her collar onto her neck.

"It's a beautiful day to be out if you like snow, but still cold. Come over here and warm up with some tea." Elizabeth indicated a small table in the corner with two chairs and a large teapot, evidently kept there for the comfort of her customers. She poured out a delicious-smelling spicy tea for Maggie, then a cup for herself, and sat down with her in the second chair.

"Business is slow at this time of day, but I've been doing inventory. I'm glad to take a break."

Maggie looked around. It was a small shop, but it made the most of its space. Besides the welcoming aroma of the tea, there were quaint touches here and there, such as a stuffed Peter Rabbit sitting on top of the children's books section, and a bowl of wooden vegetables tucked in the middle of the cookbooks. A black cat peeked out from the shelves of the mysteries. Maggie had to look twice to be sure it wasn't real.

"Dyna told me about the book you're writing. How is it going?"

Maggie winced. "It's not, I'm afraid. I seem to be setting myself up for ways to postpone starting on it." She told Elizabeth about her laptop's missing power adapter and her futile search so far to find another one.

"If you keep going up Main Street and take a right onto Hudson, you'll find O'Connell's. If they don't have what you need, I'm sure they can help you to get it."

"Terrific. Once I finally begin working, it shouldn't take me too long to put the manuscript together. It's mostly a matter of putting all my notes and ideas into plain English."

"When it's published I'll display your book prominently in the window."

"I'd like that. Perhaps with a compass or calculator next to it?"

"How about notepaper and pencils?"

"That would be even better. Maybe the book should come with them, to encourage working out the puzzles."

Elizabeth smiled. "I'll be eager to try them."

Maggie looked at her. "You know, you're the first woman

I've talked to in a long while who hasn't claimed to be just terrible at math."

Elizabeth laughed. "I guess that's going out of fashion, finally. Even the talking Barbie dolls aren't allowed to say they hate math. I never got higher than high school trig, but I always enjoyed math, liked the challenge of it." She looked pensive for a moment. "Maybe I would have majored in it, or at least minored, if I'd gone to college."

Maggie sensed a tone of wistfulness. "Something kept you from going?"

"Well, yes." Elizabeth smiled. "My mother wasn't well by the time I finished high school. She had raised me alone after my dad died when I was three, and she had a bad heart. I couldn't see letting her keep on working so that I could go to school, and nobody was offering me full scholarships, so I got a job, and eventually became manager of this store. There are living quarters attached, and it was a good arrangement, especially as Mom got worse. I could run over whenever she needed me. She died last June."

"I'm so sorry."

Elizabeth smiled her thanks, but her eyes looked tired and sad. It would be a while yet, Maggie saw, before she was over her mother's death.

"I love the way you've fixed up the shop," Maggie said, wanting to change the subject to something more cheerful.

"Thanks. I try to change the stuffed toys and things every once in a while. It gives the place a new look, and I notice the regular customers glance around a bit more, move to sections other than their usual ones."

"That cat tucked among the mysteries caught me off guard. I thought he was going to leap out any second."

Elizabeth laughed. "Some day I plan to get a real one. Won't that wake up the mystery readers, when old Blackie there winks at them?"

"Speaking of mysteries, it sounds like Sheriff Severin will have quite a time finding Jack Warwick's murderer."

Elizabeth's face suddenly flushed, and she tried to hide it by taking a sip of tea, managing only to look uncomfortable.

This surprised Maggie until she remembered Annette's cryptic comment in front of the supermarket. "Poor Mrs. Warwick and poor Elizabeth," she had said. Maggie regretted bringing the subject up. There was something about Elizabeth that made one feel very protective.

The phone rang, and Elizabeth jumped up, clearly grateful for the interruption. "Hello? Oh, Paul, hi. No, it's okay."

Maggie got up and wandered over to the children's book section to browse. With the size of the shop, though, she couldn't help overhearing most of what Elizabeth said. Paul was obviously asking about her well-being, and Elizabeth was responding with distantly polite gratitude, as she might have answered the casual inquiries of an acquaintance on the street. Maggie hadn't seen much distance in Paul's concern when he talked about Elizabeth to her and Dyna in the ski lodge, or when he had watched Elizabeth at the town meeting.

"Dinner? Tonight?" Maggie heard her say. "Thank you, Paul, but I'm really pretty busy doing inventory now. I'll probably be working late for several nights."

Elizabeth apparently didn't return the strong feelings Paul clearly had for her. She probably wasn't even aware of them, as the neutrally friendly tone of voice implied. That must cut Paul worse than outright dislike and rejection, Maggie thought.

Elizabeth hung up, and Maggie turned back to her. "Thanks so much for the tea. I won't hold you up from your work any more. I should get back to mine."

"Stop in any time." Elizabeth smiled, picking up her clipboard and pencil. She seemed to mean that sincerely.

"I will." Maggie realized she still held the slim book she had pulled off the shelf and leaned back to return it to its slot. A small spider ran out of the space and onto her hand.

"Oh!" Maggie cried, startled. She shook the spider off and was ready to step on it when Elizabeth stopped her.

"Wait, let me." Elizabeth scooped the insect onto her clipboard and carried it over to a tall potted fern near the window. "Its too cold to put him outside," she explained without a trace of embarrassment. "Maybe he'll be okay there until spring."

Maggie watched, and as she did, something clicked in her memory bank, something that had been stored there a long time ago.

"Betsy?" she said.

Elizabeth turned and looked at her. "Nobody's called me that for a long time," she said.

"Since summer camp?" Maggie asked.

Elizabeth stared at her. "You're not *that* Maggie, are you?

Maggie grinned. "I think I am. Camp, oh, what was it called, Camp Kitty . . ."

"Kittiwake!"

"Yes, that's it!"

"Girl Scout camp, down in southern Maryland."

"Right. We were in sixth grade, I think."

"The summer before sixth," Elizabeth corrected. "And we shared a cabin."

"With two other girls, Jennifer and . . ."

"Stacey." Elizabeth's eyes were dancing.

"And Stacey found a daddy longlegs on her bed once and went berserk and would have squashed it, but you rescued it and put it safely outside."

"Did I?" Elizabeth asked, smiling. "I don't remember that, but I guess I might have."

Maggie smiled back. "I wouldn't have recognized you except for the spider. You've grown up."

"As have you. That was a good two weeks, that I do remember."

"Did you stay in Girl Scouts?" Maggie asked.

"A couple more years. Then we moved, and my mother started getting sick, and . . ." Elizabeth shrugged. "What about you?"

Maggie would have answered, but a man and woman walked in the store, the bell tinkling, and the man immediately called to Elizabeth for help in locating a particular book. Elizabeth excused herself, saying, "We'll have to talk."

"Yes," Maggie agreed, and as she zipped up her jacket, she watched Elizabeth become once more the conscientious book professional. She looked up, though, as Maggie opened the door and waved farewell, and Maggie caught a glimpse of the eleven-year-old she remembered in her smile.

Maggie continued up Main Street three more blocks, fragments of the Camp Kittiwake song running through her head, then turned onto Hudson, as Elizabeth had directed. Her thoughts returned to the urgency of finding the power adapter she needed and she scanned the block anxiously for O'Connell's. It was halfway down the block, open for business, and, as she quickly found out, had what she needed. She was so relieved she could have kissed the clerk who handed the power adapter to her. Instead, she gave him her credit card, and was soon happily retracing her steps down Main.

As she passed the bookshop, she glanced in. Elizabeth was busy with another customer, but Maggie tapped on the window and held up her package triumphantly. Elizabeth grinned and did a congratulatory thumbs-up, the elderly woman in front of the counter looking up with blinking, bewildered eyes.

Maggie continued on down the street to the footpath and reentered her snowy wonderland, thinking, as she walked along, about how pleasant it was to run into someone she had known, if only briefly, in childhood. Elizabeth—rather, Betsy—must have made an impression on the eleven-year-old Maggie, because Maggie found she had many clear memories of her, mixed in with the busyness of the camp activities. They would really have to get together sometime soon and have a good laugh over it all.

When Maggie reached the cabin it was gloriously empty. Dyna, she assumed, was happily swooshing down the slopes. Maggie immediately hooked up her adapter, turned on her laptop, and spread her notes out on the round table in the living room once more. Before too long she had left Elizabeth and Cedar Hill behind and had entered a world of her own making, one that consisted mostly of numbers, and in which she was supremely contented.

She had been working diligently for several hours when she heard Dyna's car pull into the driveway. Good, she thought, she was ready for a break. She leaned back from the computer, stretching, and waited, listening for the usual shufflings of skis and boots being transferred from car to porch. Instead she heard the car door slam and footsteps pound up the steps. Maggie looked up as the door flew open, expecting an enthusiastic description of Dyna's day. But Dyna stood at the door, her mouth working soundlessly, her face a picture of disbelieving shock.

"They've been searching Elizabeth's place," she finally managed to squeak out. "They think she did it!"

Chapter Six

Maggie hovered over Dyna, who had staggered to the couch and collapsed on it, pulling off her hat to fan her flushed face.

"Tell me what's happened!" Maggie pleaded.

"I just can't believe it," Dyna said, shaking her head back and forth.

Maggie wanted to grab her shoulders and shake the words out of her. She controlled her impulse, though, chewing at her lips, and waited, giving Dyna time to come to grips with her emotions and hoping that would happen swiftly. Finally Dyna sat up straight and took a deep breath.

"I was coming off the slopes, just racking up my skis and thinking I'd take a break indoors for a while, when I overheard these guys talking. One was telling the other he just came in from town and saw "the SWAT team," as he put it, moving up Main Street. He said they were closing in on the bookstore. Maggie, this was a kid about fifteen, sixteen years old, so I figured he'd just been watching too much television." Dyna got up to throw off her jacket. She started pacing.

"Anyway, I went inside, and as I walked around I picked up a couple of whispers that sounded like Jack Warwick's name, and Elizabeth's. And that, with what I heard the guy outside say, got me plenty worried, so I threw my things in the car and drove to town.

"The Book Nook had a big CLOSED sign on it, so I went

50

into the insurance place next door. The old guy there told me he saw John and a deputy go into the book shop—no SWAT team, of course—but they stayed a pretty long time, poking around. Then he saw John drive Elizabeth away in his car and that's so awful I just can't stand it!"

Dyna stopped her pacing and looked at Maggie with a face full of distress. Maggie was sure hers looked the same. Elizabeth! That couldn't be!

"Did they find something? Is she being charged?"

"I don't know, but it sure looks bad, doesn't it?"

"How can we find out?"

"Should I call John at his office?"

Maggie thought for a moment, then shook her head. "I don't think the sheriff will be giving out information to anyone." She took up the pacing Dyna had ended, thinking hard. Dyna plopped back down on the sofa, picked up her hat, and sat twisting it, her eyes following Maggie as she moved about the room.

"Annette!" Maggie cried. "What about Annette? She'd know all there is to know, don't you think?"

"Yes, Annette! Sure she would. Should I call her?"

"No, let's go see her. Where does she live?"

Dyna scrambled to the end table that held the phone book on its lower shelf. She flipped through pages. "Radke, Raeling . . . here, Raison. Shoot, what's her husband's name? Why do they make it so hard to find women in phone books? Oh, here it is, Raison, Byron. I remember meeting him once, this total no-personality guy, and thinking, 'Byron?' They live at 238 Timber Drive. I can find that."

Maggie had already zipped up her jacket. She held Dyna's out to her. "Let's go."

Maggie jumped into Dyna's car, barely managing to buckle herself up by the time Dyna had the car in gear and had backed out of the driveway. As they drove down Hadley, Maggie's mind continued to grapple with this turn of events. Could the sheriff taking Elizabeth away mean something else? Could there be some interpretation other than the one she and

Dyna put on it? She found herself wanting that very much, even though she couldn't come up with anything reasonable.

Halfway up Main, Maggie suddenly cried out, "Oh!" Pointing, she said "There she is!" Annette stood on a corner, talking animatedly to a small group, hands gesturing and arms waving. Maggie was sure what the subject was. "I should have known she wouldn't be sitting home alone at a time like this," she said.

They pulled over, and Maggie was out of the car the instant the ignition was turned off.

Annette's round, bright eyes lit up even more as she saw fresh news-thirsty individuals approach. She waved them over as she continued to expound, clearly relishing the moment, but occasionally injecting at least a modicum of concern for the center of the excitement—Elizabeth. Maggie listened for a few moments, hearing basically what Dyna had already told her, then jumped in with her question when Annette paused.

"Do you know if they found anything in their search?"

Annette looked triumphant. "Oh yes, yes they did! Of course I wouldn't dream of imposing myself into their investigation." Maggie immediately pictured her lurking closely, eyes and ears moving like radar dishes. "But, I did happen to overhear one of them say something about a small, suspicious bottle found in a very unlikely place."

Maggie's heart sank. That sounded bad. A bottle of poison? But something was wrong. It had to be wrong. Another woman began shaking her head and moaning about the terrible things going on in the town. Maggie interrupted.

"What sent them there? What made them decide to search Elizabeth's place?"

Annette looked at Maggie, and Maggie was startled to see a certain secretiveness appear in the woman's eyes for just a moment. Was she imagining it? This was a woman who could barely wait to spread the latest news about her neighbors, good or bad. The look vanished as quickly as it appeared, though, and Annette answered Maggie's question with a hint of her usual all-knowing smugness. "Why, it must have been because of their affair. Elizabeth and Jack Warwick's. I'm only surprised it took the sheriff this long to get there."

Maggie had been tossing and turning in her bed for so long that she finally gave up and threw back the tangled covers. Not wanting to wake Dyna in case she had managed to fall asleep, she found her robe in the dark and tiptoed down the winding staircase, thinking she might have some of Dyna's caffeine-free herbal tea. They had shared a somber dinner earlier, and Maggie tried with little success to work afterward.

Rob had called and she had been happy to hear his voice and glad for the distraction. She listened to his enthusiastic descriptions of his work at the tennis camp, letting herself be lulled by what sounded like a much simpler life in the Florida sunshine. When he asked about her activities, though, she told him only of her afternoon skiing and the start of her book.

After she hung up she had a twinge of uneasiness. She hadn't been completely open with him. She tried telling herself it was only because she didn't know the whole story yet, and that it was no use telling him things in bits and pieces. But the uneasiness, along with thoughts of Elizabeth, had kept her from sleep.

Turning on just one small light in the kitchen, Maggie heated up a mugful of water in the microwave, catching the timer before it came to its ping. She let the teabag steep for a minute or two, then cradled the fragrant concoction between her hands and wandered over to the sliding glass doors. With no clouds covering it, the moon cast enough brightness on the snowy landscape to give a clear view of the woods across the road, and Maggie gazed at them, her mind busy.

Things looked bad for Elizabeth, and when more information came out they might look worse. John Severin struck Maggie as an intelligent man. She didn't think he would make baseless decisions. He must have had good cause to search the bookstore and Elizabeth's living quarters, something other than gossip, and good reason to take Elizabeth in.

But Elizabeth wasn't a murderer. Maggie felt sure of that.

Her thoughts flew back to the Elizabeth she had known so many years ago:

"Betsy, look, there's a hawk circling. I bet he's zeroing in on his prey, like Mrs. Jackson was telling us."

"Oh, I hope he doesn't get it!" Betsy had said.

"He has to eat, you know. That's how he gets his food."

"I'll feed him. I just don't want him to kill some poor little bird."

And the girls had laughed, Maggie along with them, at the image of Betsy trying to satisfy a hungry hawk with the camp's hot dogs.

Then there was the rescue of the daddy longlegs that Maggie had remembered in the book shop, something Elizabeth apparently was still doing. Most people were revolted by spiders, especially indoors. Elizabeth hovered over them.

And Elizabeth had cared for her ailing mother, even foregoing college to do it, something that clearly was a sacrifice. Could someone this selfless be a murderer?

Elizabeth had been flustered when Maggie brought up Jack Warwick, but that might have been only because of their past relationship—if they truly had had an affair—and not necessarily from guilt over his murder. Maggie suspected that Elizabeth was one of those people who agonized over things that others could rationalize away, things much less portentous than murder.

As far as the affair that Annette seemed so sure of, Maggie thought from her impression of Jack Warwick that if there had been one, he must have been the pursuer, possibly at the vulnerable time surrounding her mother's death. Elizabeth would have been an easy victim, helpless as a mouse to a cobra.

However, Annette had said a suspicious bottle had been found in Elizabeth's living quarters. If it turned out to contain the poison that killed Jack, what did that mean? Had someone planted it to throw suspicion on Elizabeth? Could Maggie live with herself if she didn't try to find out?

"Can't sleep either, huh?"

Maggie jumped and turned to see Dyna at the base of the stairs.

"I didn't hear you come down."

Dyna sniffed at the air. "Trying my lemon-ginger tea?"

"Uh-huh. It's good."

"The chamomile and mint is good for sleeping."

"I gave up on sleeping. I've been thinking."

"Yeah, me too."

Dyna looked at her, waiting. Maggie took a sip from her mug, knowing what Dyna wanted her to say. Could she? Had she made her decision? The visions of Betsy/Elizabeth she had just conjured up still floated through her head. Of course she had.

"I want to help."

"Yes! I knew you would!" Dyna rushed to Maggie and hugged her, almost knocking her over, and splashing tea on both of them. She stood back. "What about your book?"

Maggie puffed out her cheeks and blew out.

"Right now Elizabeth is a lot more important than any book, but maybe I can do both." She looked at Dyna. "With a little help. Can you stay around?"

Dyna frowned. She looked at the floor, hands on hips. "Can I stay around? Let me think. Well . . . I don't know. There's that fantastic career waiting for me in the health food store, you know. Hmmm . . ." She looked up and grinned. "Of course I can, you dodo! I'll do anything I can to help out Liz. Just tell me where to start."

Ah, Maggie thought. Where to start. It's fine to have good intentions. But to put them into action? Now that was the hard part.

Chapter Seven

Maggie poured a second cup of coffee as she chewed at her final bite of toast. After her talk with Dyna she had managed to get a few hours of sleep, which her brain apparently considered plenty since it woke her with furiously busy thoughts. The rest of her body, however, was moving much more slowly. She had made the coffee strong.

She carried her mug over to the phone and punched in Elizabeth's number. Only one number had been listed in the phone book, not in Elizabeth's name but under Book Nook. Maggie assumed it also rang in the living quarters. Wherever the phone was ringing, no one was answering. She hung up in frustration.

"Still no answer?" Dyna's voice came through cascading strands of hair as her head hung down near her knees, her fingertips reaching for the floor. Apparently having suffered fewer effects from lack of sleep, she had enough energy to practice her Soorya Namaskas. Maggie shook her head.

"I can't believe John wouldn't talk to me about it," Dyna complained. "He didn't sound like himself at all." She straightened up and flipped her hair back. Her hair stood out from the static electricity, reminding Maggie of one of those eraser-faced rubber pencils she'd had as a kid, with acrylic hair that would fly out when she rolled it between her hands.

"He was being Sheriff John, not your friend John," Maggie said. "Sometimes I guess he can't be both. Possibly he's not able to give out information on an open case." She took a sip of coffee. "I wonder, though, what his own feelings on this situation are? Does he really think Elizabeth is guilty?"

"If he does, he won't be my friend anymore." Dyna ran her fingers through her hair, calming it only slightly. She now looked, Maggie thought, like an enthusiastic rock-band drummer, minus the tattoos. Maggie's hand went to her own hair. After her restless night she probably didn't look much better.

She got an idea. "Why don't I call Paul Dekens? I wouldn't be surprised if he's managed to get in touch with Elizabeth." Dyna's face lit up in agreement, and Maggie picked up the phone.

A female voice at the ski lodge answered Maggie's call. "Paul's outside right now. Can I have him get back to you?" Maggie hesitated. "Will he be there for the next hour or so?"

"Yes, I'm sure he will. We're having trouble with one of the lifts. He's out there with the crew."

"Great. I mean, that's too bad. But thanks." Maggie hung up and turned back to Dyna. "If we drive over to Big Bear we should be able to talk to Paul face-to-face."

"Sounds good. Just let me change into something warmer. Oh, and maybe I better do something with my hair."

Maggie didn't answer. She was already halfway up the stairs to do the same.

Maggie sat at the edge of a metal chair in front of the desk in Paul's office, Dyna on one next to her. She had had to remove a stack of papers from it first, which now lay lopsidedly on the floor beside her. Paul came in, bringing cold air with him, his face red from the wind. He zipped off his jacket and tossed it into the corner of the small room nearly filled by the cluttered desk. "Carol said you've been waiting to see me?"

He looked at Dyna as he said it, but Maggie answered. "It's about Elizabeth." His face clouded over.

"We're sure she's being framed," Maggie hurried to explain, "and that she needs help. But we can't get hold of her.

We hoped you might be able to fill us in on what's happening."

Paul sat down in his chair and leaned back slowly. "You're right. She needs help. But I can't seem to convince her of that."

"You've talked to her then?"

He nodded. "I wanted to get her a lawyer, to pay for him. She refused."

"Has she been charged?"

"Not yet. She feels since she's innocent, there's no chance of being charged and therefore no need of a lawyer."

Maggie nodded. Elizabeth was being naive and trusting, very much like Maggie had expected. "Do you know what they have on her so far?"

"Elizabeth told me they found a small, clear, unlabeled bottle containing a small amount of liquid at the back of a kitchen cabinet she seldom uses. There was also a paperback book on poisons, with a bookmark at the section on household poisons. She says she never saw either before."

"Does she keep the doors to her apartment locked?"

"The back door, yes, but not the one that opens off the shop. It's at the back of the shop, out of view from the front register."

"So if she were busy with a customer, someone could slip in to her place?"

"Exactly." Paul's face looked grim.

"But John must know that," Dyna put in.

Paul's eyes shifted back to Dyna. "He must, but until someone can say they actually saw that happen, he has only the facts of the bottle and the book to deal with. They must be testing the contents of that bottle right now, and if it contains the same poison that killed Warwick, Elizabeth will be in serious trouble."

"Well," Maggie said, "then our job is to find out who put those things there. Do you know of anyone who would want to do this to Elizabeth?"

"I can't imagine anyone wanting to hurt her like this, but

whoever killed Jack Warwick wanted to cover his or her own butt. Elizabeth probably seemed the most vulnerable."

Maggie nodded. Her own thoughts precisely.

Maggie sat behind the wheel of her car, silent and staring forward.

"What are you thinking?" Dyna asked.

Maggie turned towards her. "Lots of things, one of which I don't like very much."

Dyna's eyebrows went up questioningly.

"Paul seems like a good guy, wanting to help Elizabeth. But we both know he had a very good motive for eliminating Jack Warwick himself. If the poison used was a common one, something found in the average household, as the bookmark seems to indicate, then it's likely available to anyone. He also must have been to Elizabeth's apartment a few times, been somewhat familiar with it. It's very possible he could have planted those things in Elizabeth's cabinet to cover himself."

Dyna's face looked pained. "But he loves her. You told me that yourself, and I think you're right. He couldn't do such a thing to someone he loves."

"I hope not. For Elizabeth's sake. She doesn't need any more betrayal. We can only hope he didn't decide he loved Big Bear even more." Maggie took a deep breath. She thought about what to do next. "Well, we really need to talk to Elizabeth. Why don't we drive over to her place, pound on the door, and make her let us in?"

"Got the battering ram in the trunk?"

"Of course. But only to be used if necessary."

"Aye-aye, captain," Dyna responded, saluting briskly as Maggie put the car in gear.

It turned out they didn't need a battering ram against the door, just a few light taps of Maggie's knuckle on Elizabeth's window. Finding, as expected, the book shop closed and dark, they had followed a trampled path in the snow around to the back. Maggie peered in and saw Elizabeth sitting with her back to the window in an overstuffed chair, wrapped in an afghan, feet drawn up. She appeared to be staring at a blank television, and her head turned slowly at the sound of Maggie's taps.

Elizabeth pulled herself out of the chair and opened the door.

"May we come in?" Maggie asked. "We need to talk." She took Elizabeth's silence as assent and she and Dyna kicked off their boots, padding in on sock feet as Elizabeth stood aside.

The kitchen/sitting area felt bleak to Maggie, although with its braided rug and pillow-strewn chairs it should have felt cozy. It must be Elizabeth's mood filling the room, she thought. She looked at the kitchen counters, which were clean and bare.

"Have you eaten today?" she asked.

Elizabeth appeared to have to think about it. "No," she finally said, "I guess I haven't. I'm not sure when I ate last."

Dyna pulled open the refrigerator door. "There's some eggs here. How about I scramble you some?"

Elizabeth smiled a little. "You don't have to take care of me. I'm all right."

She looks anything but all right, Maggie thought. "Sit down," she directed. "I'll fix some tea." A small canister near the sink yielded a bag of the same spicy tea that Elizabeth had served Maggie the day before, and she put a mug of water in the microwave. Dyna cracked eggs into a frying pan and popped some bread in the toaster. Between the two of them they set a hot breakfast before Elizabeth in a short time.

A little color came back to her cheeks as she ate, and Maggie smiled at Dyna's chatter about nothing, which she was sure helped Elizabeth relax some. Elizabeth polished off her plate, obviously hungrier than she had realized, and Maggie began washing up as Elizabeth sipped at her tea. Dyna found a box of cookies and brought it over, pulling one out for herself.

"Have you heard anything from John since yesterday?" Maggie asked from the sink. Elizabeth shook her head.

"Did he give you any idea how things stood as of last night?"

"No, but I'm sure he realizes those things he found in my kitchen weren't mine." She said it with a vagueness that told Maggie she was refusing to face the situation.

"Did he actually say so?" Dyna asked, a look of hope on her face.

"Well, no. But they're not. They're so clearly not."

Maggie put down her dish towel and came over to Elizabeth. She sat down on the hassock near her. "Elizabeth, you know they aren't yours, and you can tell John they aren't yours, but you can't prove it. They were found here in your kitchen. A book on poisons. And a bottle whose liquid may prove to be the poison that killed Jack Warwick. Unless someone else's fingerprints are found on those items, which I very much doubt will happen, you are in a very bad situation. Dyna and I want to help you, and we will do everything we can. But you will have to help yourself too."

Elizabeth stared at Maggie for what seemed like a long time. Finally she put her mug of tea down and said, "What should I do?"

Maggie took a deep breath. "First, call Paul Dekens and tell him he can get you that lawyer." When Elizabeth started to protest Maggie held up her hand to stop her. "I know you're innocent, but that's all the more reason to have a lawyer. If the District Attorney starts putting together a case against you, you've got to have someone on your side."

"But I can't let Paul go to that expense. He needs every penny to keep Big Bear afloat."

"Let him do it. Maybe you can pay him back later. We'll worry about money later." To herself, Maggie thought that if Paul was innocent himself, he would be doing it out of love and wouldn't mind the expense. If he was guilty and just playing Mr. Nice Guy, well, then the more it cost him the better. Maggie would check out the lawyer herself to make sure he was competent.

"Next," she continued, "think very hard and tell me if there is anyone who you think would set you up like this."

Elizabeth looked down at the floor, and Maggie saw her pale face take on tinges of red. She looked back at Maggie.

"I can't really imagine anyone doing that. But then I couldn't imagine anyone murdering Jack, and someone did. If I had to guess as to who would want to hurt me, it would have to be Leslie, Jack's wife."

Elizabeth's eyes had filled with tears at this, and Maggie knew they were not tears of anger but sorrowful tears of regret. She could almost read what was going through Elizabeth's mind. Apparently Dyna could too, for she grabbed one of Elizabeth's hands.

"Hey," Dyna said, "I know you probably feel rotten over the affair, but don't go thinking you deserve the chair for it. Someone else killed Jack, not you, and someone else is going to pay for it. Got that?"

Elizabeth wiped her eyes. She pulled a tissue from her pocket and blew her nose. Then she smiled up at Dyna. "Got it."

Back in the car Dyna looked over at Maggie. "Do you think she'll be all right?"

"She's coming around. Tomorrow we can take over some groceries—her cupboard looked pretty bare. Then maybe we can talk her into reopening the book shop. She needs to stay busy."

And I need to add a few more pages to my book, Maggie thought. She hoped she could squeeze in a couple of hours of work later on that night. But for the moment she would concentrate on the murder.

"Where to now?" Dyna asked, as Maggie turned on the ignition.

"Where else," Maggie said, "but to see the one person Elizabeth could bring herself to suspect. Mrs. Jack Warwick."

Chapter Eight

Maggie pulled up to the large, Federal-style house.

"Is this it?" she asked Dyna.

"I'm pretty sure it is. I remember Annette telling me at the town meeting that the Warwicks had rented the old Kirby place, the best house in town that was available."

Maggie stepped out of her car and looked at it thoughtfully, taking in the character and gentility the home exuded and wondering just how well Jack Warwick had fit into it. She climbed the few steps with Dyna to knock at the door.

Leslie Warwick answered it herself, looking surprised but pleased to see them. She was dressed in form-fitting pants topped with a bright green silk shirt that set off her tawny hair beautifully. Not exactly mourning clothes, Maggie thought, but then what exactly *were* mourning clothes anymore, and who wore them except to the actual funeral?

"How wonderful to see y'all," Leslie said, stepping back to welcome them in. "Don't worry about your boots, just come on in. It seems like ages since I've been able to really talk to anyone. Mrs. Hanson!" Leslie shouted, causing Dyna, who stood closer to her, to jump.

A grey-haired woman in a navy dress who must have been Leslie's housekeeper bustled into the foyer and took their things. Worry lines creased her face, but she smiled pleasantly when Maggie handed her her jacket with thanks.

"Come in, come in," Leslie sang cheerily, her voice lilting

in the Southern accent Maggie had forgotten about, and led them into a formal living room decorated mainly in white, with a touch of icy blue. "Let's get comfy. What can I get y'all to drink?"

Maggie noticed for the first time that Leslie had a glass in her hand, partly filled with ice cubes and a dark amber liquid. Iced tea? Maggie hoped it was, considering the time of day, but Leslie's manner seemed livelier than simple tea would induce. Maggie also remembered Leslie's unsteadiness at the town meeting.

Leslie stood at a portable bar, waiting for their answers. "Pepsi is fine for me," Maggie said.

"If you have mineral water I'd like that please," Dyna said.

Leslie wrinkled her nose but smiled and rooted around to find the items. "This cart reminds me of my days with the airline, pushing one down the aisle, smiling, smiling, smiling." She dropped ice cubes into Maggie's glass, poured her drink into it, and held it out to her.

"You were a flight attendant?" Maggie asked, taking the glass.

"For a while. I thought I would see the world. What I saw was a bunch of airport terminals. After that I did some modeling.

"Evian all right?" she asked Dyna, who nodded. It was on a photo shoot out on Long Island that I met Jack. We were doing an advertising brochure for one of his companies, I forget which one. I just remember shivering in a bathing suit on a chilly beach in October. Anyway, he swept me away from it all, and I've never had to work a day since."

Leslie smiled when she said it, but Maggie thought she detected a touch of wistfulness in her voice. Leslie took a long drink from her glass.

"We should have come before, to offer our condolences," Maggie said. She sat down on a white brocade sofa that sank under her weight about as much as a rock would, and she blinked with surprise, causing Leslie to laugh.

"When I said 'Let's get comfy,' I forgot where we'd be sitting. The furniture in here is all for show." Leslie carried her glass to one of the stiff-looking chairs and sat down, pulling her feet up. "The only really comfortable stuff is in Jack's study—nice, soft leather—but I just can't bring myself to go in there."

"We understand," Dyna said, looking sympathetic.

"Oh, don't worry, I'm not going to break up in tears or anything. It's just that the whole situation is so . . . so weird. They won't even release his body yet. Jack wanted to be cremated, and they're telling me they're not finished with it yet—tests and all, you know."

Maggie nodded. She took a sip of her Pepsi and out of the corner of her eye saw something move. A cat, tiger-striped and muscular, had slipped through a partially-opened glass door that appeared to lead to a solarium, and was marching firmly towards Leslie.

"Mrs. Hanson!" Leslie shouted. "He's here again!" She looked distinctly uncomfortable.

Mrs. Hanson scurried into the room, all apologetic. "I'm so sorry, Mrs. Warwick," she said, in what sounded to Maggie like a slight German accent. "I was sure I had closed him in the den. I don't know how . . ."

"Just get him out of here."

Leslie's vehemence surprised Maggie. The cat didn't look particularly vicious, and in fact hung limply in Mrs. Hanson's hands when she scooped him up and carried him away.

"He's Jack's cat," Leslie said, as though that explained everything. "He found him in an alley somewhere and brought him home, called him Ali. I swear he fussed over him more than I've seen him do for any other livin' creature. *Any* other. He knew I didn't like cats, but . . . oh, never mind. I'll get rid of him, somehow." She grinned. "Would y'all like a cat?"

Maggie saw Dyna's eager intake of breath, and before she could blurt anything out said, "We can't. We're just staying at the cabin for a short time. No way. Sorry."

Leslie shrugged. "It's okay. Maybe Mrs. Hanson knows someone."

Maggie's gaze wandered back to the room the cat had been in, an idea forming. "Is that a solarium?" she asked. "Could I take a peek at it?"

Leslie looked over her shoulder in surprise, as though she

had forgotten the room existed. "Sure. It's nice and cheery in there, but the wicker furniture really isn't any more comfortable than this stuff."

"No," Maggie said, "I can see some greenery in there, and I just love plants." Dyna looked at her with an odd expression, which Maggie ignored as she popped up and followed Leslie to the sun room. "Oh, isn't it lovely, Dyna," she said, cringing inwardly as she heard herself sound just like one of her mother's gushy friends. "How do you keep them so healthy?"

Leslie shrugged again. "I don't take care of them. They came with the house and Mrs. Hanson waters them, I guess."

Maggie wandered around the room, which was bright and sunny, and with its tropical decor was a stark contrast to the bare trees and snow visible through the windows. She bent down to sniff a blooming camellia. "Mmm, wonderful." A tall palm stood in its pot nearby. "I could spend all day in a room like this. Doesn't it make you want to stretch out in a swimsuit and soak up the sun?"

Leslie was about to say something when Mrs. Hanson's voice sailed in, calling, "Mrs. Warwick. It's the caterer. Shall I have him call back later?"

"No, I'd better talk to him. Excuse me," she said to Maggie and Dyna. "I'll just be a minute."

The moment she left the room, Maggie hissed to Dyna, "Stick close. I'm going to take samples." She immediately began breaking off parts of each of the plants in the room.

"What are you doing?" Dyna whispered, wide-eyed.

"I'll explain later." Maggie broke off a piece of the potted palm. "How can we carry these? I don't have a purse. Did you bring one?" Maggie tested the pockets of her jeans, which fit closely, and found they wouldn't hold more than a leaf or two.

"No, I hate purses," Dyna said. "I don't know. Wait, put them in here." Dyna held out the front pocket-pouch of her hooded sweatshirt, and Maggie quickly shoved the twigs she'd gathered into it. By the time Leslie returned, the pouch had been fully packed, and Dyna kept a hand at each side to keep greenery from slipping out. Maggie thought the look on her face was priceless, a combination of "Who, me?" innocence, and "Please don't ask me to shake hands" worry. She would have laughed if the situation weren't so serious.

They followed Leslie back to the living room where she immediately freshened her drink. "That was Dan Morgan. He's doing the food for the fundraiser."

"Fundraiser?" Maggie asked.

"Yes, weeks ago Jack and I agreed to hold a fundraising buffet dinner here to benefit the school. They need a new library, and Jack, of course, was looking for ways to ingratiate himself with the town. It's gotten a lot of promotion ever since, and I don't see any reason not to go ahead with it."

She really doesn't see any reason, does she, Maggie thought.

"I don't suppose you knew about it, but everyone will be here. The PTA ladies are handling the ticket sales. I hope you'll both come? It's the day after tomorrow."

Maggie nodded, slowly. "I guess . . ." She looked over at Dyna, who sat looking a little plumper than she had when she first arrived, her hands still stuffed into each side of her pouch.

"Sure," Dyna said, nodding stiffly. She seemed afraid of talking too much, as if taking in the extra breath needed would call attention to her lumpy tummy.

Leslie didn't seem to be noticing much, though, her thoughts on other things. "The food will be wonderful, since Dan's doing it. Have you ever tried his wild mushroom soup? It's out of this world. I always ordered it when we ate at his restaurant. He sent some over after, well, after, you know, that town meeting, which was so kind of him, don't you think? Anyway, there'll be loads of flowers. And music. We'll move the baby grand into the . . ." Leslie suddenly screamed as Ali, the orange cat, appeared from nowhere and leaped up onto her lap.

"Get off! Get off!" She had partially risen from her chair, but the cat stubbornly refused to jump off, his claws anchored firmly in her clothing. "Mrs. Hanson!" Maggie stood up to help and had just about pried him loose when the housekeeper appeared at her shoulder to take him from her.

"I was in the laundry room, Mrs. Warwick," she explained, agitated. "I don't know how he gets out! He's like a demon cat."

"A demon, yes! He's a devil cat. I won't have him around me! I won't! He's Jack's cat. I've seen his eyes. He's watching me! Jack is watching me through him."

"Wow," Dyna said, as she buckled herself into Maggie's front seat. "What was all that?"

They had taken their leave, Leslie apologizing for her outburst but clearly too overwrought for their company anymore. Dyna had managed to get her jacket on without losing much of the clandestine contents of her sweatshirt, gracefully picking up a single twig that had fallen to the floor as Maggie distracted their hostess at the door.

"I don't know." Maggie frowned as she looked at the house, then put her key in the ignition.

"Sounded like a guilty conscience to me, wouldn't you say?" Dyna asked.

"Maybe. Whatever she was sipping might have had a lot to do with it too."

"Could be. And maybe she was sipping whatever she was sipping because of a guilty conscience. Anyway, now that we're out of there," Dyna patted her middle, "how about explaining what all these plant pinchings are for? You're not going to start your own greenhouse, are you?"

"No, but I want to take them to a greenhouse or a garden center. Someplace where they can identify them for me."

"You're suddenly interested in botany?"

"I'm interested in plants that can kill. Poisonous plants."

"Oh, wow, you mean like hemlock? Do you think Leslie was growing hemlock to poison Jack?"

"I don't think anything yet. That's why I want to get these identified. It's just one possibility that occurred to me after that cat came out of the sun room. Remember Paul said the book found at Elizabeth's was marked at the chapter on household poisons? Well, plants are in a lot of households. Maybe one of these are poisonous. Now, where can we go to find out?"

They stopped at an outdoor phone booth that had, miraculously, it seemed to city-bred Maggie, a directory hanging in it, and checked the address of a garden center Dyna had thought of. She then pulled out a map and directed Maggie a few miles out of town.

Maggie drove into a large, mostly empty parking lot, surrounded by an open area that in warm weather must have been filled with flowers and shrubs, but now was filled with snow. A large, glass-roofed building stood before them, and when they entered Maggie immediately felt an increase in heat and humidity. She had to shield her eyes from the bright glare coming through the roof, and when her eyes finally adjusted she saw a long, narrow interior filled with rows of tables. Indoor plants, potting soil, and varieties of plastic and ceramic pots filled the tables and much of the floor. A lone clerk sat next to the cash register. She put aside a book and looked up expectantly.

"Hi," Maggie said. "I need someone who is a plant expert. Would that be you?"

The young woman grinned and shook her head. "That'd be my dad. I just help out here on the afternoons I don't have classes."

"And I take it you're not majoring in botany?"

The woman laughed. "Uh-uh. Accounting. All I can tell you is how much the merchandise costs. Dad's gone to Plymouth to pick up some things. He won't be back for two or three hours, at least.

"Do you think if I left these here," Maggie asked—Dyna had begun pulling out plant pieces from her sweatshirt, causing the young woman's eyes to widen—"he could identify them for me?" She wrote down the phone number at the cabin. "I'm interested in plants that could be poisonous, in any way." Seeing the frown that formed on the girl's face, she quickly added, "My sister, here, is expecting a baby, and we don't want to have anything around that could be harmful."

"Oh, I understand. Kids always put the darndest things in

their mouths, don't they? I'm sure Dad would be glad to help. I'll just put these in plastic bags until he gets back."

"Thanks so much," Maggie said.

"I'm having a baby?!" Dyna's aggrieved whisper into Maggie's ear made her flinch as they pushed out the door of the greenhouse.

"Shh, sister dear," she whispered back. "Mustn't upset your hormones."

"It's bad enough I *looked* pregnant back at Leslie's with the front of my shirt all stuffed up. Now you're telling people I *am* pregnant." She was grumbling, but Maggie knew it was just for show.

"Dyna, after this is all over, I promise to go around and explain everything. Right now, I'm starved. In case you haven't noticed, we never had lunch, and it's almost dinner time. How about stopping somewhere?"

Dyna brightened up at the mention of food. "I was just thinking the same thing. I could feel my blood sugar starting to go down."

"Yes," Maggie said with a sly grin. "We mustn't let that blood sugar get too low, you know, now that you're eating for two." She sidestepped away from Dyna's kick, and jumped into the car.

"Just for that remark, I'm going to insist on going to my favorite place," Dyna said, as she climbed into the passenger seat.

"Oh, where's that?"

"Leslie reminded me about it, talking about the catering she's having. Dan Morgan's restaurant."

Maggie frowned. "I was thinking of someplace we could get dinner in a hurry. I need to hit the books tonight."

"Morgan's won't be busy on a week night. And he's the only place that carries vegetarian selections. I promise, we'll get quick service."

Maggie pondered as she put the car in gear. The things they had back in the cabin's refrigerator would take some time to prepare, she knew. Besides, her stomach had started growling.

If they were seated quickly at the restaurant, at least there'd likely be breadsticks to nibble at.

"Okay," she said, backing out of the parking space. "Just tell me the way." She promised herself after the meal she would put aside all thoughts of the murder for several hours, and immerse herself completely in "Math Games and Puzzles," even if she had to do without another night's sleep.

Chapter Nine

Maggie stood in the foyer of Morgan's and looked around, impressed with the atmosphere of the place which, despite a certain formality, managed to have a cozy feel to it. She wondered how that had been achieved.

"You should have been here a couple years ago," Dyna said. "What a difference. Early-seventies dowdy. This is a transformation."

At that moment a hostess appeared, menus in hand. A fiftyish, slightly plump and friendly-looking woman, she smiled at Dyna's comment. "Karin Dekens did the decorating. She started working on it shortly after the Morgans took over. She put on the final touches just a few weeks ago."

"The Morgans?" Maggie asked. "Dan is married?" She remembered seeing him at the town meeting during the growing debate. He had sat silently alone.

The hostess, whose name tag read "Vickie," grimaced. "I should be more careful about that. Brenda Morgan was killed a year ago, in an accident. I was hired to take her place here."

"Killed! How sad," Dyna said. "What happened?"

"She was driving alone, late at night on icy roads, when she apparently lost control of the car and crashed into a tree. Dan was devastated."

With Dyna looking close to tears, Maggie said, "How brave of him to carry on with a business they must have planned together."

"Yes. I'm sure it's what Brenda would have wanted. Dan's immersed himself in this place ever since. It's been his life. I'd like to see him get out a little more, but," she added with a smile, "his customers certainly appreciate his dedication. His specialties always get raves. Table for two?"

Vickie led them to a table near the large fireplace, and after mentioning a few items not on the menu, left them to decide.

"See, I told you we'd be seated right away," Dyna said.

Maggie nodded, still taking in the atmosphere of the place. Decorated in blues and beiges, the room had a colonial theme that didn't jump out at you but slowly snuck into your consciousness. She liked it. And she liked being near the fireplace, which had a low fire glowing in the grate, the smell of hickory barely discernable. Pewter pieces graced the mantel above and antique-looking prints decorated the walls.

The few patrons on this weeknight were scattered widely at the other tables, and she recognized Regina White at a corner table with two companions. Maggie's attention having been diverted by the room itself when she first entered it, she now realized that she had passed by the Dekens family— Karin, Alexander, and their young son Ethan—and her gaze settled on them.

"I can't decide between the eggplant Parmesan or the herb-cheese omelet with sun-dried tomato," Dyna said.

Maggie hadn't even looked at her menu, and quickly began scanning it. "The beef bourguignonne sounds good."

Dyna wrinkled her nose, and Maggie countered with, "I'll need the protein to get my brain cells working on my book tonight."

"What you'll be getting is a lot of fat."

"Well, my brain cells will need some fat too." Maggie knew a lot of what Dyna said about diet made sense, but she also knew she wasn't ready to give up foods that still had an emotional, sentimental hold on her. She had grown up in a family that ate pot roast and had backyard cookouts on Sundays. The smell of smoking hamburgers or steak always carried pleasant memories with it. Then there were the teenage group trips to McDonald's or the local pizza place. How could she give up the good feelings those foods still gave her? She couldn't, was the answer, so she decided on beef bourguignonne.

A young waitress came and took their orders, and Maggie picked up a breadstick from the basket she had left behind. As she nibbled at it, her gaze returned to the Dekens' table. So Karin had decorated Dan Morgan's restaurant. Maggie remembered seeing Karin and Dan deep in conversation at the town meeting, shortly after the meeting adjourned. She also remembered Alexander walking by, his lips curling unpleasantly as he looked at the two, and she wondered what exactly that meant.

Alexander's face had a flushed look to it tonight, and he reached for his wine glass after each bite of food, which necessitated refilling it often. Karin's face had the studied lack of expression Maggie had seen before. Only Ethan, their four-year-old, seemed to be enjoying himself, murmuring quietly to himself as he lined up peas on the edge of his plate.

"Regina's over there in the corner with some of her picketers," Dyna said, breaking into Maggie's thoughts. "Now that Jack's gone, I wonder what they could be planning?"

Maggie glanced over at Regina's table. The older woman's expression looked just as fierce as she conversed with her companions, as it had during the debate at the town meeting. Maggie suspected, though, that Regina carried the same intensity into most areas of her life. She could picture Regina discussing the likelihood of snow coming with an "argue to the point of death" approach.

"I wonder," she said to Dyna, "if Jack's departure will actually be the end of Regina's or Paul Dekens' problems, as far as Big Bear is concerned. I've been thinking about it, and it's possible Jack's power in his company may just be passed on to others, who might continue to follow the course he set."

"I hadn't thought of that."

"You keep playin' with your food like that, son, and you'll make the famous Chef Morgan mad." Alexander's voice came loudly from his table, his words slurred. "You don't wanna get someone with a room full of meat cleavers mad."

Maggie's attention, as well as that of the entire room's,

flashed to Alexander. He tipped his chair back on two legs, then drained his wine glass in a single gulp. Ethan had frozen in his little game, and stared wide-eyed at his father. Karin reached over and brushed a few stray hairs from her son's forehead, murmuring something softly.

Maggie looked back at Dyna, who raised an eyebrow at her, but as their waitress arrived at that moment with their dinners, neither said anything. The normal conversations of the room gradually resumed, and Maggie turned her attention to her food.

Vickie was winding her way slowly through the tables, exchanging pleasantries, when she neared the Dekens' table.

"Why don'cha ask Chef Morgan to come out and join us?" Alexander called out to her, an unpleasant grin distorting his face. "There's a chair right here for him, right next to Karin." He kicked it out several inches with his foot as if to prove his point.

Vickie answered genially that Dan was very busy and asked if they'd care for dessert.

Karin shook her head no, her dark hair swinging softly, and began gathering their things. She offered a last drink of milk to Ethan and rose to help him off his booster seat, avoiding looking at her husband or the other diners. Ethan immediately ran to the foyer, stopping to play with a large spinning wheel that sat in a nest of potted plants.

Alexander stood up unsteadily, scraping his chair noisily.

"Hey Chef Morgan," he called out, "your decorator's leaving. Don'cha want to come out? Give her a nice big hug?"

The door to the kitchen slapped open, and Dan Morgan emerged, wiping his hands on his white apron, a dark scowl on his face. He spoke quietly to Karin, who had gone up to him, and she shook her head. Maggie caught some of her words: "It's okay. I'm sorry."

Karin took her husband firmly by the arm and led him to the foyer, he stumbling and protesting that she hadn't said a proper good-bye to her special friend. Somehow she managed to get the three of them out the door, leaving behind a room of uncomfortable diners, some pretending nothing had happened, others exchanging knowing looks and muttered comments with their companions. Dan Morgan pushed back into his kitchen without another word, and gradually the level of noise in the room returned to normal.

"Poor Karin. I had no idea," Dyna said, poking at her omelet with her fork, looking distressed.

"Annette told you Alexander had gambling debts. Looks like he has other problems too."

Dyna just shook her head. "Poor Ethan," she said, and pushed a forkful of omelet into her mouth, chewing glumly.

Maggie watched, realizing she'd have to distract her somehow or Dyna would be up all night with indigestion. She searched her mind rapidly and pulled out a subject that was never far from reach.

"By the way, I've been struggling with a section in my book lately. Maybe you can help. Would you mind?"

Dyna looked up. "Help you on your math book? I don't know anything about math, you know."

"Yes you do. I need to know if I'm explaining something clearly enough. Would you listen to it? Tell me what you think?"

"Sure. Go ahead." Dyna forked some lettuce into her mouth and munched, her gaze no longer returning to the door through which the Dekens had just departed, but fixed on Maggie, some of the distress in her eyes replaced with a flicker of interest.

Maggie told her about the magic square, quoting the directions as closely as possible. Since she had worked the explanation over at least a dozen times, it wasn't hard to do. "Does that make any sense to you?"

"Yeah, I think so." Dyna turned her fork around and drew with the rounded end on the tablecloth. "What you're saying is you divide up a square into nine small squares, and pick different numbers to put in them." She tapped her fork on the table into her creased squares. "And the numbers in each row have to total up to the same thing no matter what direction you go in. This way, this way, that way . . ." Her fork made horizontal, vertical, and diagonal swipes on the table cloth. "Is that right?"

"Yes! You got it." Maggie beamed at her, and Dyna beamed back.

"I guess that means if I understood it, some elementary school kid's gonna get it too, huh?"

"Dyna!" Maggie said, exasperated. She hated it when Dyna put herself down like that. She had just drawn a breath to say so when someone's loose sleeve brushed her shoulder in passing, distracting her.

"Sorry," the woman apologized, pulling her jacket tighter to her. Maggie smiled an "it's okay," recognizing one of the people who had been sitting with Regina. Regina followed in a moment, buttoning up her pea coat. She stopped at their table, looking down at their plates.

"Good," she fairly grunted to Dyna. "I see you're continuing to take your diet seriously." Her words were approving, but anyone hearing only the tone or seeing her face might have thought she was scolding Dyna. Maggie wondered what it would be like to truly be on the receiving end of Regina's wrath, and hoped she'd never find out.

"Yes, Regina, I've been cutting out meat for nearly a year now. Have you met my friend Maggie Olenski?"

"Saw you at the town meeting. How do."

Maggie shook the firm hand Regina held out to her. She felt uncomfortably on the edge of a squirm as she noticed Regina glaring at her plate of beef bourguignonne, but a flash of annoyance brought out her stubbornness instead. She speared a chunk of beef and popped it into her mouth, smiling benignly up at her critic as she chewed. Regina continued to glower, but Maggie thought she caught a glint of amusement in her eyes before she turned back to Dyna.

"You came to the right restaurant for a good choice of vegetarian meals. Had to convince him," Regina tossed her head in the direction of the kitchen, "it was in his own best interests to add them, but he did a good job on it once he got going."

Maggie wondered what form Regina's "convincing" had taken, and how she managed to persuade Dan Morgan, who looked like he had a stubborn streak of his own, to do something he might not have originally intended. She was picturing the two matching glare for glare when Regina broke into her reverie.

"You two hear about the school's fundraising dinner?"

"Uh-huh," Dyna answered, "today, as a matter of fact."

"You can buy tickets from me, if you like. I wasn't going to be involved, with it being at the Warwicks' home. But now it's just *Leslie* Warwick, I don't mind. It's a good cause, you know." Regina smiled for the first time, and Maggie wasn't sure if it was in honor of the good cause, or at the thought that now there would be one less Warwick in attendance.

Maggie realized she wanted to find out more about this woman and she spoke up before Dyna could respond. "We would like to help the school. As a teacher myself . . ." Maggie paused and saw Regina's face immediately show approval, as she knew it would. Everyone she met since she received her teaching degree seemed to react the same favorable way, which was pleasant, but would have been even more pleasant if that approval had extended to voting for increased teachers' salaries. She continued, "I understand the often dire needs of schools. Can I stop by and get the tickets from you tomorrow?"

Regina nodded. "Of course. I'll be home in the morning. You know my house?" She raised her eyebrows inquiringly at Dyna.

"Sure, right up there at the top of Fernhill Road?"

Regina nodded, twice this time, since it apparently also signified her good-bye. "Not before eight," she said as she turned and walked away, jamming her knit cap over her grey hair before she pushed through the outer door.

"Eight?" Maggie repeated, to Dyna.

"She goes out hiking before sunrise—even in the winter!"

"Hmm. Maybe vegetarian does have its merits," Maggie said, but grinned quickly to show it was a joke.

"So we're going to Leslie's fundraiser," Dyna said. "Have you thought about what we'll wear? This sounds like a fancy function."

"Oops. I sure didn't pack anything remotely fancy. Well, we'll figure something out." Maggie finished up her dinner, resisting an urge to mop up the last of the delicious sauce, and asked Dyna if she wanted dessert. She fervently hoped she didn't because she was anxious to get back to the cabin. Dyna must have picked up on the vibes because she shook her head, puffing out her cheeks at the same time as if to prove she was full enough. Maggie asked for their check and before long they both rose from the table to leave.

As they paused in the empty foyer, zipping jackets, Maggie looked down at the greenery that hugged the antique spinning wheel. "Does any of that look like what was in Leslie's sun room?" she asked Dyna.

"I don't know. It all looks the same to me. Are you going to pinch some of this too?"

Maggie glanced around. Vickie was across the room, engaged in conversation. Diners were occupied with their meals or with each other, not paying attention to them. She bent to reach for a twig when the outer door suddenly pushed open and the mayor and Susan Larson stepped in. At sight of them Susan immediately sang out, "Well, hello! How nice to see you again."

Maggie straightened up and snapped her hands behind her back. "Hello," she said, knowing her face probably said, "I wasn't doing anything," and she struggled to neutralize it. She recalled having spoken with Susan Larson at the town meeting, just before Jack Warwick had slumped to the floor, and tried to remember what they had talked about. She was spared having to come up with a conversation opener, however, when Susan and Tom alternately congratulated them on having chosen this fine restaurant, asked how they had enjoyed their dinner, and launched into a catalog of their own favorites. Vickie appeared with menus and the older couple followed her, still talking amiably, but now directing most of it to the seated diners they encountered as they progressed. By then more new customers had arrived and Maggie reluctantly gave up on finger-pruning Dan Morgan's plants that night.

"Maybe we'll hear from our plant expert and at least find out what's growing in Leslie's indoor garden," she said, following Dyna out the door. She pulled her collar up against the chilling wind and hurried toward the car.

Chapter Ten

As she pulled up in its driveway, the cabin looked forbidding to Maggie for the first time, the unlit windows looking down at her with ominous gloom. Maggie felt a shiver go down her back, but told herself it was the cold, the short ride from the restaurant not giving the car enough time to warm up. Dyna's car was tucked cozily in the small garage, but hers had to remain outside. After she and Dyna climbed out, she locked her car for the first time since she had come there, something she always did back in Baltimore but had felt unnecessary until now in Cedar Hill.

The uneasy feeling dissipated once she was inside the cabin and Dyna flicked on the switch, flooding the downstairs with light and chasing away the goblins. The first thing Maggie did was inspect the answering machine. The message light blinked.

"I hope that's our plant expert," she said, tucking her gloves into the pocket of her jacket and hanging it up. The warmth of the cabin was comforting. She pulled off her boots and padded to the phone. There were two messages, and when Maggie punched the button the machine told her the first had come at 5:36 P.M.

"Oh, ah, Miss Olenski. This is Dave Fortier. I'm calling about the plant specimens you left with my daughter. Most of them are just fine, but I'd get rid of the oleander if there'll be small children around. It's extremely poisonous. All parts of

81

it. That's the one that has narrow leathery leaves with big, white or pink flowers. You can call me back here until six if you want more details. Or tomorrow will be fine."

Maggie looked at Dyna, who hovered over the other side of the answering machine.

"Wow," Dyna said. "Leslie could have done it, then."

"If Jack Warwick was poisoned by oleander. We don't know that yet. But we can talk to John, tell him what we found, and maybe he will have gotten the toxicology results."

"I bet it will be oleander. It has to be. Leslie has a whole slew of motives to kill her husband. And you saw how guilty she was acting. And she has this poisonous plant right there in her house. Nothing could be more convenient."

"I agree, there seems to be a lot pointing to her right now. But let's wait for the final report before we jump to conclusions."

Maggie pushed the button for the second message. It was Rob.

"Hi," he said. "It's me. Sorry I missed you, 'cause I'm going out soon. I'll try again if it's not too late."

The machine beeped off, and Maggie made a face, her shoulders slumped in disappointment.

"Gee, that's too bad," Dyna said. "You missed a call from Rob."

"Oh, well. Maybe we can catch each other later." Maggie turned briskly away. "It's probably just as well. I've got to get some work done." She headed over to her laptop and flipped on the switch. As it hummed and beeped through its booting up process, she began sorting through her papers.

"I'm just going to fix some tea to take upstairs with me, and then I'll be out of your way," Dyna said. She put a mug of water in the microwave, then started rummaging around the cupboards. "Didn't we buy some Oreos?" she asked.

"I thought you were stuffed."

"I am. I just want a little taste of chocolate."

Maggie smiled. "It's a good thing chocolate isn't an animal protein, isn't it?" Dyna had long ago confessed she was a chocoholic, but unashamedly and with obvious relish. Dyna grinned, still rummaging.

Maggie couldn't resist a little more teasing. "You know there's caffeine in chocolate, don't you?"

"Don't even say things like that," Dyna said, putting her hands over her ears. "I didn't hear it." She found her cookies and tucked the package under her arm, carrying her tea mug in both hands. As she stepped carefully up the wrought-iron stairs she called over her shoulder, "If it's true—and it isn't— the holistic theory is that a very little of the bad stuff brings out the good stuff in you. Or something like that. And if chocolate has caffeine, which it doesn't, it's very little."

Maggie laughed. Another example of what she called "Dyna logic." She watched Dyna disappear into her room, then turned back to her papers, determined to put all thoughts from her mind but math-related ones. It wasn't easy. Thoughts of Rob intruded. When she pushed them away, images of Leslie fixing poisonous brews crept in.

Oleander. Had there been a plant like that at Dan Morgan's? She tried to remember, but not having been looking for it specifically at the time, the appearance of the various plants didn't sink in enough to recall. Did it matter, though, she wondered, if Dan Morgan kept a poisonous plant, not among the supplies of his kitchen of course, but decorating his foyer? Yes, it did, she answered herself. Because everyone who had been at the town meeting had to be a suspect for now. Regina had been there, and certainly had a motive for murder. And tomorrow morning she would go to see Regina. What could she find out from her?

"Stop!" Maggie ordered herself. "Math Puzzles and Games. What you need to find out is how to start Chapter Five. Worry about murder tomorrow." She heard the crinkle of Dyna's Oreo package from above, and the taste of the chocolate creme-filled cookie immediately flooded her mind. Maggie sighed. Writing, she thought, would be a lot easier if one's brain had little switches that would turn certain parts off. She looked at her computer screen which waited blankly for her to fill it with words. And a switch, she thought wryly, to turn the part you needed on.

The next morning, Maggie tried to coax Dyna out of her Oreo-induced lethargy by pulling back her flower-printed comforter and shaking her. She had already called her twice, with little response.

"Wake up. We have a busy day ahead of us."

Dyna pulled the comforter back, snuggling into its warmth, but opened up one eye towards the window.

"It's not even totally light out," she protested. "Regina's probably still out walking somewhere."

"I think we better see John first thing. Tell him about the oleander."

Dyna moaned. "John's probably still asleep too."

"I doubt it. C'mon. By the time you're downstairs, I'll have breakfast ready.

Dyna groaned a few more half-intelligible things which Maggie decided she didn't want to have repeated, then dragged herself to a sitting position and rubbed at her face. "Never, *ever*, start watching *Terms of Endearment* with a full package of cookies at your side." She swung her feet to the floor and held her stomach. "Just tea and toast for me."

"Okay. Dress warm. The wind is howling out there." Maggie heard a final groan as she trotted down the stairs.

Dyna got herself together in a surprisingly short time, after all her groaning, and to Maggie's satisfaction they were on their way to the sheriff's office within forty-five minutes. Unfortunately, the lone deputy there informed them within seconds of their arrival that John was out.

"It's just some kids done some minor vandalizing, though. I woulda gone, but Dottie particularly wanted John. You could probably catch him at her coffee shop, if you want to."

Maggie did want to, so they backtracked to Main Street, pulling up behind the sheriff's car parked in front of the coffee shop. John stood beside a cracked window with a grey-haired woman. She was talking agitatedly with much arm-waving and pointing and he was listening patiently, an open notebook in hand. He looked over as Maggie turned off her ignition, flipping his notebook closed. The woman said a few final words, then tramped into the shop.

"Morning," John said, as Maggie climbed out of her car. The wind had calmed down somewhat, but was still brisk enough to make her glad she wore a hat.

Dyna swung her door closed and called, "You get started early." It was a statement, but Maggie thought she detected an undertone of complaint, perhaps from lingering thoughts of the warm bed she had been dragged out of due to John's disagreeable work hours.

"Two certain young criminals," he gestured towards the cracked window, "got started even earlier. Fooling around with icy snow balls, I suspect. Forgot how hard they can be. Dot said they took off like two bats out of hell when it happened."

"Are they in big trouble?" Dyna asked.

"Mostly with their parents. I'll have to drive over and tell them about it. Dot, the way she feels right now, would like to have them sent up the river, but she'll likely be satisfied with a replacement window. The kids will be shoveling a lot of snow this winter to pay for it, I'll wager."

"Before you go," Maggie put in, "can we talk?"

John looked at her, possibly gauging the seriousness of the talk, and suggested they have a cup of coffee inside.

The shop had a long counter where two men in wooly ear-flapped hats sat, the only customers at the moment. They turned a fraction on their stools and nodded to John as he passed. He led Maggie and Dyna to a booth near the back where they all piled in, John calling to Dot for two cups of coffee, "and a cup of . . . ?" he looked at Dyna.

"Just orange juice for me," Dyna said, wisely, Maggie thought. She could imagine the likely reaction of Dottie and the two ear-flapped patrons to a request for rose hip or hibiscus flower tea.

Maggie waited until their order came, then told John what she had discovered in Leslie's sun room.

"Ah, it's there too," was his surprising response.

"So you knew about it. Was oleander the poison that killed Jack Warwick, then?"

"What were you doing in Leslie's sunroom?" he asked.

"Investigating, of course," Dyna said. "We know Elizabeth didn't kill Jack Warwick. You don't really believe she did either, do you?"

"Investigating?" John repeated, a scowl forming on his normally impassive face.

Maggie uneasily recalled her earlier assurance to him that she wouldn't play private investigator. But everything had changed since then. She didn't want to go into it all right now, and simply asked, "You said 'it's there too.' Where else is it?"

"The foyer of Morgan's restaurant, for one."

"Oh," Dyna said. "Maggie wondered. She almost snitched a piece of his plants, but the mayor and his wife walked in."

John gave Maggie a look that pushed her to defend her actions. "I don't think I'm interfering with police work, just trying to come up with anything you might not have thought of. Obviously you thought of checking Dan Morgan's foyer."

"Yes, he has an oleander plant there."

"So maybe he made the poison that killed Jack," Dyna put in, looking quite satisfied to Maggie. Leslie or Dan, it clearly didn't matter to Dyna which, as long as it wasn't Elizabeth.

"He could have. Half the town could have too," John said. "Dan told us, and Vickie confirmed it, that all his foyer plants were trimmed a few days back, and the clippings dumped in one of the cans out back. So much they overflowed it. The cans stand next to a well-used alleyway. Anyone could have come by and helped themselves, if they knew what to look for. Including Elizabeth," he added.

Dyna's face fell. "But she wouldn't have, you have to know that, John."

"I can't get into that."

"Elizabeth may be getting a lawyer," she said. "Paul Dekens said he'd help her get one."

John merely nodded at this.

"May I ask," Maggie said, "what was it that sent you to

search Elizabeth's place? You haven't searched anyone else's, as far as I know. Why hers?"

"Elizabeth's lawyer, whoever that is, will be informed that we had the proper search warrant issued for probable cause." John took a long drink from his coffee mug. "Elizabeth had a motive to kill Warwick. You probably heard the gossip." Maggie nodded. "A prosecutor could do a lot with the 'rejected woman seeks revenge' argument. You're right, though. Several others who were at that town meeting had good reasons for wanting Jack Warwick dead. But we didn't get a tip from a certain concerned citizen about happening to stumble upon some rather incriminating evidence in anyone else's kitchen cupboard."

"A certain concerned citizen! Who? Who are you talking about?"

John stood up and pulled bills from his pocket to cover the tab. "That, for now, is the business of the authorities, which, it seems I need to remind you, you are not one of."

John put his hat on and gave Maggie a hard look. "In other words, Miss Olenski, a murder investigation is serious business, not a game. Stop playing Nancy Drew and leave the police work to the police."

John turned and walked out, leaving Maggie to stare after him. She felt her anger at his words slowly warming her cheeks before the cold outside air, let in by his exit, reached her booth with its chill.

Chapter Eleven

"Nancy Drew?" Dyna said, her face a picture of indignation that Maggie was sure hers mirrored.

New customers had come in with questions for Dot about her cracked window. These provoked agitated responses, and the noise level in the small shop grew rapidly.

"Let's talk about it in the car," Maggie said, and she slid out of the booth, followed quickly by Dyna.

John's car was gone, its parking space now occupied by a tan pickup. Maggie climbed over the snow bank at the curb and into her Cavalier, Dyna slipping at the same time into the passenger seat.

"How could he say that to you?" Dyna asked, buckling up with clumsy fingers. Maggie watched the fumbling, unsure if it was caused by the thick gloves Dyna wore or the agitation John seemed to have stirred up.

"He's the sheriff. He has every right. It *is* his job, and he was just telling us that," Maggie answered. She didn't know if her explanation was to calm Dyna or herself. To be accused of playing games had stung. She wasn't playing. Maggie felt she understood the seriousness of the situation as much as anyone. It was only because she was completely convinced of Elizabeth's innocence and the danger she was now in that Maggie had gotten involved. She took a deep breath, realized the air in the car was quite cold, and turned on the ignition.

"Let's not worry about John for now. What do you think of that piece of information he gave us?" she said.

"About the concerned citizen tipping him off?"

"Yes."

"That was weird. Who could it have been?"

"I don't know." Maggie rubbed her hands, which even in their gloves were beginning to feel the cold. She looked at the car's heater, willing it to start blowing warm air.

"The murderer!" Dyna said, her eyes growing wide. "The murderer could have planted the bottle and the book in Elizabeth's cabinet, then called John anonymously to tell him where to look."

Maggie thought about that. "Maybe. But John didn't say it was an anonymous tip. He said it was a certain concerned citizen. I don't think John would have acted on an anonymous tip, do you? So he must have the identity of this citizen. Would the murderer take a chance of putting himself in the spotlight like that?"

"No," Dyna admitted reluctantly, "probably not, if he had to give his name and all. John could think he—or she—had actually put the stuff there."

"So who did call?" Maggie asked. "Who, as John, said, 'happened to stumble' on this incriminating evidence, and felt guilt-free enough to report it? Who was poking into Elizabeth's cupboards?"

"We were," Dyna said. "But that was later, you know, after John had already been there, when we were fixing her breakfast."

"So someone was in Elizabeth's kitchen, very soon after Jack Warwick was poisoned. Maybe doing the same thing we were, cooking up a meal for Elizabeth. She must know who that is."

"Let's go ask her."

"Yes, eventually," Maggie said, "but I'd like to go to Regina's right now. Catch her before she hurries out and try to talk to her a bit while I get those dinner tickets from her."

"So drop me at Elizabeth's. No, drop me at the supermarket.

I'll pick up some supplies for her like we were talking about, then I'll have a good long talk with her."

"Can you carry bags of groceries there?"

"No problem. I guess you don't have the layout of the town in your head yet, but the market's just a couple blocks away."

Maggie thought about the route they had taken that first morning to get to the supermarket, most of it coming back now. Dyna was right, the market wasn't too far from Elizabeth's. "Well, that would save some time, if you don't mind." It occurred to Maggie that besides restocking Elizabeth's bare kitchen and with any luck learning who had called John, Dyna's buoyant spirits might also help lift the depression that probably still hovered there. "I'll pick you up on my way back."

"No, no," Dyna flapped her hand, "I'll walk back, through the path. That way we can both take as much time as we need." As Maggie put the car in gear and pulled into the traffic lane, Dyna asked, "What do you think? About what I should pick up for Elizabeth, I mean?"

"I don't know if she's vegetarian or not, if that's what you're wondering. She needed milk, maybe some fresh fruit, a few frozen dinners." She glanced over at Dyna and said, "Oh, and she might like a nice big package of Oreos."

Dyna shook her head firmly. "Uh-uh. After last night I don't even want to look at those things."

Maggie grinned and wondered how long chocoholics managed to stay on the wagon. It occurred to her that food cravings were certainly inconvenient, at best, and unhealthy at worst. As she braked for a stop light she reached for one of the sourballs in her console and unwrapped it, thinking how fortunate she was to be free from addictions like that.

Maggie stood at the door of the large old house. It wasn't what she would have expected for an older single woman like Regina. With a huge Victorian-style veranda, three full floors, and a spacious yard, the place clearly required a lot of upkeep. From what Maggie could see so far, it had been getting it. She wondered how Regina managed.

She pressed the doorbell and heard an echoing "bing-bong." It was several seconds before the door was pulled open, and Regina stood before her, her small frame three-quarters wrapped in an immense white apron, impatiently beckoning her in.

"I'm in the middle of something in the kitchen," she said by way of greeting, and turned on her heel to lead the way, walking Maggie through a dim hallway with rooms on each side. Maggie caught glimpses of heavy draperies and dark, old fashioned furniture. The kitchen, when they reached it, wasn't much cheerier, but did at least welcome her with pleasant aromas.

"Fixing a couple casseroles to take that Kerr woman," Regina said, as she resumed her place at a cutting board that had a mound of chopped onion on it. Several small zucchinis and an eggplant sat beside the board, and Maggie saw a bowl of beans nearby.

"Elizabeth?"

Regina nodded. "Saw her this morning when I was out walking. Doesn't look good, probably not eating like she should. Can't blame her, with all that's going on."

Maggie's first thought was how considerate that was of Regina, but she instinctively refrained from saying so, sure that Regina would look on it as merely the sensible thing to do and anyone who didn't automatically think so was an idiot.

"Help yourself to some coffee." Regina jerked an elbow in the direction of the coffeepot. "I'll get those tickets for you in a second."

"Take your time. I'm in no hurry." Maggie picked up a mug that sat beside the pot, glad that she had an opportunity to dally a while. She had been afraid Regina would meet her at the door with tickets in hand, and she wouldn't get two words out of her.

Regina resumed chopping, doing it as rapidly and efficiently as Maggie thought she must do just about everything in her life. She mixed ingredients and seasonings in a large baking dish, grated cheese over the top, and slid it into her oven, all the while lecturing Maggie on the vitamin and mineral content of each component, and the superiority of this kind of meal over the average American dinner.

Maggie watched and listened without comment, taking an occasional sip of what turned out to be delicious coffee. When Regina wiped her hands and sat down at the large oak table opposite her, Maggie asked, "Was Elizabeth out walking so early too?"

"Don't know exactly what she was doing. Maybe just getting a breath of air when she knew most townspeople wouldn't be out and about."

Maggie nodded. "I'm glad she is getting out. Was this the first time you've seen her since the town meeting?" she asked, thinking she might as well narrow her list of possible "concerned citizens."

Regina looked at her sharply, and grunted with a quick nod. Maggie thought that was quite likely the truth. If Regina had found the book and bottle of poison—and hadn't planted it there herself, of course—Maggie couldn't picture her simply calling John and waiting for him to do something about it. She would almost certainly drag Elizabeth by the hair to the sheriff's office herself. The question that remained, however, was if Regina had planted the evidence herself.

"Since you're making this casserole for Elizabeth, I assume you have some sympathy for her situation, the fix she's in."

Regina snorted. "I have little sympathy for someone who fools around with a married man. But Jack Warwick was a manipulating charmer, a predator. Going after that young woman, the state she was in after her mother's death, was akin to child abuse in my opinion. He was a rogue, a devil who deserved what he got."

"But you don't think Elizabeth poisoned him, do you?"

"Don't know. Don't really care who did poison him. All I know is she's in a heap of trouble right now."

"Yes, she is. And she's going to need a lot of help."

"Best help she can get at this point is a good lawyer."

"I agree," Maggie said emphatically.

"Tom Shaeffer." Regina said this as if stating the obvious.

"Tom Shaeffer?"

"Lawyer. Best in the county. She should get Tom Shaeffer."

The phone rang and Regina stood up to answer it. It seemed to be someone on the school fundraising committee with questions about the logistics of the dinner, which Regina responded to with brusque, precise answers. When she hung up she said, "I'll get those tickets for you. Two?"

Maggie nodded, and Regina left the room, returning in seconds with a large brown envelope. She pulled out two tickets and remained standing as Maggie wrote the check, sending the clear signal that her break was over and their conversation was ended.

As they walked back down the dim hallway Maggie searched for something to keep Regina talking, and, glancing in the living room, commented on the furniture. "Are they antiques?" she asked.

"Most of the things were my grandmother's," Regina said, pausing at the doorway of the room, her expression softening half a degree. She patted the door frame. "This house was built by my grandfather, and my family has lived here ever since. We've had wealth, but we never sought it. We always gave back to the community. Cedar Hill flourished through the years largely because of us, and Jack Warwick would have destroyed it in weeks."

"Cedar Hill means a lot to you," Maggie said.

"I know some think of me as a foolish crusader, but my causes have always been for the good of the town and its surrounding environment. Any clear-thinking person could see what Warwick's plan would do to this place, and any clear-thinking person who cared about his life here would have spoken up against it. As the last of the White family, I've always tried to continue its tradition."

The last of her family. How bleak that sounded to Maggie, and simply to strike a more cheerful note said, "Your grandfather built a lovely home."

Regina nodded. "I keep it up as best I can, even the guns in that case over there, which my father, Lord forgive him, used for hunting. People weren't as enlightened about such things as they are now."

"Opinions certainly do change on things that were accepted in another age," Maggie said.

"More opinions need to change concerning the environment," Regina said. She moved toward the door again, and Maggie had no choice but to follow. "The fools of this town who were ready to trade the beauty of it for a few dollars from Warwick need to examine their priorities." She opened the front door and stood aside for Maggie. "This fundraising dinner, at least, is a good thing. People working together for the right cause." Having said her final words she put a hand on Maggie's back and guided her firmly out the door.

"Yes," Maggie said. She would have added more but the door closed on her before she could draw a breath. "It is," she said out loud to herself, and laughing softly, walked down to her car.

Back at the cabin, Maggie mulled over what Regina had said. She seemed to have the right motives for all she did—for the good of the town—although certainly not all the townspeople agreed that what she did was good for it. Lacking family of her own to occupy her, she clearly put her energies into the preservation and promotion of Cedar Hill. How far, though, would Regina go for this passion of hers? If murder were the only way to prevent an evil to her beloved Cedar Hill, would Regina murder? Maggie hadn't seen any plants in Regina's house, but according to John, anyone could have acquired oleander clippings if he or she knew what to look for. Regina struck her as someone who would find out plenty about anything she needed to know.

Maggie looked at the clock, surprised that Dyna wasn't back yet. Maybe she should have stopped at the book shop to pick her up. Then again, perhaps Dyna and Elizabeth were having a good long talk. It would be great if that were the case. Maggie thought she might as well squeeze in a few minutes' work.

She sat down at the computer and soon her mind was filled with math as she maneuvered through a world of numbers. She hadn't been working too long before the phone rang.

"Maggie, it's me," Dyna's voice came through the receiver,

sounding distressed. "Can you come pick me up? I'm at the vet's."

"The vet's? What are you doing there?"

"It's Ali. Leslie's cat." Dyna's voice began to crack with emotion. "I found him in the woods. He's in pretty bad shape. I think maybe he was poisoned."

Chapter Twelve

"Okay, now tell me how this all happened," Maggie said, as she and Dyna left the veterinary clinic and headed for her car. She had waited patiently as Dyna got an update on Ali's condition from the veterinary staff and their plans for treatment. She'd even waited without complaint when the receptionist insisted on telling them both the long, sad tale of her own cat's recent illness and demise.

"Oh, Maggie, it was so pitiful," Dyna lamented as she climbed into the Cavalier. She waited until Maggie got behind the wheel and buckled up before continuing. "I had just come onto the path from Main Street when I saw Ali up ahead, just standing and looking at me."

"You're sure it was Ali?"

"Uh-huh. Besides being the same size and color, I recognized the collar he was wearing when we were at Leslie's. A kinda glitzy thing with rhinestones. I remember thinking that it really didn't fit a former alley cat and that he seemed embarrassed about it. Anyway, I stopped and called to him, and held out my hand, but he kept on standing there, looking kinda, you know, dazed. Then he threw up—and I mean threw up—everything, not just a hairball."

"Cats do that, I hear." Maggie had started the car and was heading back to Hadley Road.

"I know. My Missy used to spit up hairballs all the time, and at the first wheeze we'd scoop her up and put her outside

96

on the grass until it was over. But when it was, Missy was always fine. Ali, when it was over, keeled over and just laid there, his eyes all glassy-looking. Maggie, it was awful!"

Dyna had painted a vivid picture, and Maggie felt a pang for the innocent creature, deathly ill in the cold, snow-covered woods. "How did you get him to the vet's?"

"I just grabbed him and ran back to the street, waving like a crazy person until Susan Larson pulled over and picked us up."

Very brave of Susan, Maggie thought, to take a sick cat into her car, but very kind of her too. Maggie was sure Dyna would have run all the way to the vet's with the ailing feline if she had to. They reached the cabin, and Maggie pulled into the driveway.

"What did the vet say?" she asked as they opened their doors and started climbing out of the car.

"All he can say for now is that it might have been something Ali ate. He's treated Ali in the past and knows he was a healthy cat."

"So he doesn't know yet if it was poison of some kind?"

Dyna followed Maggie up the steps and into the cabin. "No, but he thinks it's pretty suspicious, I can tell." They pulled their jackets off and yanked at their boots, Dyna hopping on one sock foot as she tugged. She finally sat down on the floor of the small foyer, making it necessary for Maggie to climb over her. "I mean, just the look on his face," Dyna continued as she scrambled back up. "And he knows Leslie doesn't like that cat."

"You think Leslie might have poisoned Ali?"

"Of course! She wanted to get rid of her husband, she had oleander in her house, and now Jack's dead. She wanted to get rid of her cat, and Ali almost died."

"Will Ali be all right?" Maggie sat opposite Dyna at the other end of the sofa.

"Yeah, I think so. I asked them to call me if there's a problem."

"Shouldn't the vet call Leslie? Ali's still her cat, you know."

"No way! She's not getting another chance at him."

"Dyna, I think you're jumping to conclusions. First of all, we don't know yet what made Ali sick, and second, there's no proof that Leslie killed her husband or tried to kill her cat."

"But who else would want to kill the poor thing. I mean Ali, not Jack. Lots of people wanted Jack Warwick out of the way, but only Leslie hated the cat. We saw that ourselves."

"Well, let's see what the vet comes up with, if anything. And we should probably talk to Leslie and see what she has to say."

Dyna had crossed her legs, and her right foot was bouncing faster than Maggie's pulse while her fingers drummed on the end table next to her. "Whatever she says, she's not getting that cat back. I'll take him, as soon as he's well enough to come here."

Maggie sighed. She knew Dyna meant it, and she understood and wasn't about to try to discourage her. But it looked like one more complication was about to be added to her on-going struggle to finish the book she had come up here to work on.

"Tell me about your talk with Elizabeth," Maggie asked. "How is she doing?"

Dyna's foot slowed down, and the tempo of her drumming fingers gradually went from frantic to simply rapid. "Lizzie's doing a little better, I think. At least she laughed when I walked in with all the groceries. She helped me fix a couple of sandwiches and we talked a while as we ate them."

"Did you find out who might have called John about the things in her cupboard?"

Dyna nodded, a small grin forming. "We should have figured it out."

"Who?"

"Take a wild guess."

Maggie looked at Dyna, thinking, until a light went off in her head. "Annette?"

"You got it. Elizabeth says Annette came over the day after the town meeting with a small coffee cake. Said it had been accidentally left behind when she loaded up her car with things for the meeting the night before. Annette claimed she was on a diet and Elizabeth would be doing her a favor to take it off her hands. When Liz was busy with a customer, she asked Annette to go back to her kitchen for a knife so she could slice it and put it on her tea table in the shop, and invited Annette to have tea with her. But when Annette came out a few minutes later, she was suddenly in a big hurry, didn't have time for tea, babbled about having to go somewhere, and rushed out."

Maggie nodded. "We should have known."

"What a snoop."

Maggie grinned. "She'd make a good detective, wouldn't she?"

Dyna looked over at her and grinned back. "Maybe we should sign her up."

"To what? The Maggi-Dy Investigative Agency?"

"I was thinking more Dyna-Mag."

"That sounds too much like the name of a vacuum cleaner, wouldn't you say?"

"And Maggi-Dy sounds like, well, we'll have to think of something better."

"I think we'll have to think of something better to do with ourselves after this is over. But until then," Maggie stood up, glad to see that Dyna's mood was back to normal, "and with the goal of reaching that happy state as soon as possible, I think I'd better make a phone call or two."

Maggie picked up the receiver of the cordless phone next to Dyna and carried it over to the kitchen counter. Sitting on one of the high stools, she punched in the number of Big Bear, waited to be put through to Paul, then asked him if a lawyer had been retained for Elizabeth yet. She wrote down the name Paul gave her, a small frown forming, and asked how Paul had chosen him.

"Judd Ambler's good," Paul assured her. "He was highly recommended by someone who knows lawyers."

"Someone told me Tom Shaeffer was the best around here."

There was silence for a moment, until Paul said, "Tom wasn't available. Judd will take good care of Elizabeth."

What was Maggie hearing in Paul's tone now? Was it anger at her challenging his choice? Or was it simply the tension of someone who cared about Elizabeth and was distressed at the situation she was in that required the services of a lawyer? Maggie couldn't say for sure. After getting Judd Ambler's number, she ended the call, thanking Paul for his help.

She sat for a moment, thinking, then punched in another number. Her brother Joe answered, and Maggie smiled at the sound of his voice. She remembered how long it had taken him to finally forgive her for getting involved in the murder of last summer, and decided not to risk his good humor by explaining what she was doing now that was taking time away from the book she had come to Cedar Hill to write.

"I thought I'd catch you between classes today," she said. "How's it going?"

"Maggs! Hey! It's going great. How about you?"

"It's pretty cold up here, but it's great skiing. You'll have to come up some time."

"Yeah, as soon as I'm self-supporting and have some spare change."

"You'll get there. Joe, you know that law office you worked in last summer? Do you think they'd be able to check up on a lawyer for me? A guy up here in New Hampshire?"

"Yeah, probably. I could ask. What do you need it for?" A hint of suspicion had crept into Joe's voice now, and Maggie hastened to remove it.

"It's just a friend of a friend up here needs a lawyer, to handle a situation where she's absolutely not to blame, and I'd like to make sure she gets a good one." Maggie gave him Judd Ambler's name, and Joe seemed to accept her explanation without pressing for more details. She hadn't lied to him, she told herself, pushing away the twinge of guilt she was feeling. What she had said was absolutely true, if not the whole truth. And she wasn't in a court of law, after all.

They talked a bit about his studies—Joe was working towards a master's in political science at the University of Maryland—and about their parents, whom Joe still lived with. This, he claimed, was a financial necessity, but Maggie suspected he also liked the convenience and the home-cooked meals. Joe was a bright guy, but fairly laid back and not as eager to assert his independence as Maggie had been.

"Oh, I almost forgot," Joe said. "Your editor called."

"My editor! Yikes! What about?"

"I think she wanted to know how the book is coming. I told her where you were, and gave her the number up there. Is that okay?"

Okay? That meant she'd probably be calling here soon, wanting a progress report. Maggie felt her stomach lurch as she thought of the looming deadline and the work she still had to do. "Sure, Joe, that's okay," she said, knowing he assumed she was spending every waking minute at her computer. How could she tell him she'd been getting behind on her book in order to investigate another murder?

Maggie ended the conversation and returned the receiver to its cradle, her hand still resting on it. How quickly could she vacate the cabin, she wondered, and be out of reach of the dreaded editor's call? It seemed she had barely formed the thought when the phone rang, vibrating under her hand.

Maggie yipped, pulling her hand away as if from a hot iron, and jumped back two feet. The phone rang again.

"Want me to get that?" Dyna asked, poking her head out of her room upstairs.

"No! Let it ring. Let the machine get it."

After the fourth ring the machine clicked on, and after the beep Maggie heard that familiar voice calling from New York, friendly, but at the same time steely, the voice of someone Maggie suspected few tried to cross or contradict.

"Maggie, Anne Striker here. Just checking in on how the manuscript is shaping up. Call me at . . ." Maggie had tuned out by then, visions of ripping the phone cord out of the wall going through her head even as she realized how infantile she was being. She couldn't avoid the woman forever. After all, she had paid Maggie an advance and deserved to check up on her once in a while. But not yet. No, not yet.

Dyna trotted down the steps, a look of curiosity on her face.

Maggie glanced at her and slumped down into the sofa. "Don't ask," she said.

Dyna shrugged and dropped into the plump chair opposite her. "I still can't get over John being so rotten this morning over our trying to help. I mean, I thought he was a pretty neat guy. Today he acted like, like my *father*, for gosh sakes."

Maggie thought of the stern look on John's face at the coffee shop as he warned her to stay out of official business. It still made her nostrils flare. She had never taken kindly to orders. They tended to make her want to do the opposite. That had certainly been the case last summer, after Joe found out what had happened at the resort and demanded she come home immediately from her ill-fated vacation. It had only strengthened her resolve to stay.

John Severin wasn't her younger brother, of course. And his warning carried a little more weight. But unless he planned to arrest her and lock her up, Maggie didn't see what he could actually do to stop her from investigating. She had presumed, naively it seemed, that she and John could work together somehow, cooperate, but clearly that wouldn't be the case. Now she could only hope to get inside information from Elizabeth's lawyer—with Elizabeth's approval, of course—and bypass the forbidding Sheriff Severin.

Her thoughts went back to her visit with Regina, and she realized she hadn't shared any of it with Dyna yet. As her mind ran over it she sat up with a start, remembering something.

Dyna looked up from the fingernail she had been examining. "What?" she asked.

"Something just occurred to me. Something bad."

Dyna's fingernail went to her teeth as she waited.

"If the vet finds that Ali was poisoned with oleander, the same poison that killed Jack, things might look even worse for Elizabeth."

"What do you mean?"

"Ali was outdoors, and probably ate whatever it was this morning. Regina had been out walking early this morning and said she saw Elizabeth out too."

Dyna looked at her blankly, not getting it.

"Don't you see?" Maggie asked. "Elizabeth, who's been keeping out of sight, was outdoors early today, probably at the same time Ali was out. The same time Ali might have been sniffing and looking around, like the good alley cat he is, for something to eat."

Chapter Thirteen

"Maggie!" Dyna protested, "Elizabeth would never poison a cat!" The look of horror on Dyna's face was so awful Maggie hurried to explain.

"I didn't mean she did, Dyna. Of course I know she wouldn't have poisoned Ali. I only meant that it could look suspicious to the wrong people."

"But she doesn't have the bottle of poison—if that's what it was—anymore. John carried it off after his search, remember?"

"I know. But the darn plant seems so available in this town. They should probably change the name from Cedar Hill to Oleander Ridge."

"Ha! You're right. There could be a bottle of oleander extract tucked away in every cupboard, for all we know. What's that old slogan—'a chicken in every pot?' Maybe Cedar Hill's should be 'poison in every cupboard.' "

"What I'd like to know," Maggie said, "is who put that particular bottle and that book on poisons in Elizabeth's cupboard."

"I asked Elizabeth who could have slipped them in there, and she has no idea. She says the Book Nook was so busy just before Christmas that anyone could have gone into her living area without her knowing. She says she's never worried about keeping her door locked, always trusted the people here."

Maggie nodded. "Annette's a possibility, of course. But since she seems to be the one who called John about seeing it, I think that takes her out of suspicion, don't you?"

"Yeah. Like we talked about before, if she was the murderer, she wouldn't want to put herself in the picture that way. Besides, I think Annette gets her kicks poking into what other people are doing, not by doing it herself."

"So who do we know of so far as a possible?" Maggie began ticking off her fingers. "There's Paul Dekens. He has a motive to kill Jack Warwick—to keep Big Bear—and probably the opportunity to hide the bottle in Elizabeth's cupboard."

"Oh, I really hope it's not him," Dyna said. "Count Leslie twice for an extra good motive for being married to a rat that cheated on her, and for having the poisonous plant growing in her own house. I don't know if she ever went to Elizabeth's book shop though. She doesn't seem like a reader, does she?"

"She could have bought books for someone else, if not for herself." Maggie touched a third finger. "Dan Morgan had oleander too, in the foyer of his restaurant, and his motive might be to preserve his business, which could go under if the ski resort was sold."

"Yeah, maybe," Dyna agreed, with less force than she had shown for Leslie. "And there's Regina, you know."

"Right." Maggie pressed a fourth finger. "She said herself she had no use for Jack Warwick, and hated what he proposed to do to the town."

"What about Alexander and Karin?" Dyna asked.

"Well, Alexander wanted to sell Big Bear to Jack Warwick, so that probably lets him out. Karin, however, sided with Paul. She and Alexander don't seem to agree on very much, as far as I can see."

"Yeah. If Alexander was the one poisoned, everyone would sure be looking at Karin with suspicion. But you don't think she would have killed Jack, do you?"

"She doesn't seem like the type, but I don't think we can eliminate her just yet. She did have motive, and she was there at the refreshments table and certainly had the opportunity."

"I guess," Dyna agreed, somewhat reluctantly. "But let's prove it was Leslie, okay?"

Maggie laughed. "We'll try to prove it was whoever it was, and just hope it's not someone we've grown to like."

"I know," Dyna said, not echoing Maggie's laugh. "It would be a real bummer for that to happen, wouldn't it?"

Maggie looked at Dyna's face with a twinge of concern. Dyna had been the one urging her at the beginning to get involved in this murder investigation. And Maggie knew Dyna was as convinced as she of Elizabeth's innocence. But what if the murderer turned out to be someone who would be nearly as upsetting as Elizabeth? Things didn't always turn out the way you wanted them to, and Maggie wondered if Dyna would be able to handle it if they didn't. Would it be better to get Dyna away from all this? Maggie resolved to think about that very seriously.

Concern about Dyna still lingered in Maggie's mind when she woke up the next morning. She had stayed up late, working on her book so that she would have the best possible report to give Anne Striker when she called the editor that day. She promised herself to do it as soon as the working day began at the publishing house in New York. With a little luck, she thought, Anne would be unavailable and she would be able to get away with leaving a message.

"Wow! It snowed last night!" Dyna's voice carried down the hall from her room. Maggie jumped out of bed and pulled her window curtain aside to be greeted by a vision in white. Several inches of snow had fallen while they slept, covering the cabin's formerly clear walkways and weighing down tree branches.

"It's beautiful!" Maggie cried, delighted with the dazzling whiteness softened only by blue-grey shadows of trees in the path of the sun.

"Beautiful, yeah," Dyna said from Maggie's doorway. "But they probably won't get around to plowing Hadley Road for quite a while, and we need to do some shopping."

"We do?"

"Tonight's the fundraiser at Leslie's, remember? Do you have anything remotely wearable for a fancy dinner hanging in that closet?"

Maggie looked at the closet door, knowing the only things behind it were jeans, casual tops, and a fuzzy bathrobe. "Nope."

"Me neither. And we're going to have to figure out how to get to a dress shop or end up walking around that dinner looking like two pathetically dressed detectives trying to eavesdrop on everyone's conversations."

"Instead of looking like two well-dressed school fund supporters trying to eavesdrop on everyone's conversations?"

"Exactly."

Maggie grabbed her robe and trotted down the steps to the living room. She stepped into her slippers, one at a time, as she hopped over to the sliding glass door that faced Hadley Road and their driveway. Looking out, she saw that the snow was definitely too high for either her Cavalier or Dyna's rental Ford to maneuver, as it came nearly up to the cars' bumpers.

"Will it even be plowed in time to get to the dinner?" Maggie asked.

"Oh, sure. They'll clear it by then. They're much faster in Cedar Hill than in Baltimore because they get snow here all the time. But they have to do all the main roads first, you know. Hey, I've got an idea!"

Maggie looked at Dyna warily. "You're not going to suggest we turn the draperies into ball gowns, are you?"

"Huh? Oh!" Dyna grinned and made a face. "No, we're in Cedar Hill, not Tara. I was thinking of cross-country skis! We've got all the equipment here. We can just ski through the woods over to Main Street."

"You make it sound so easy."

"It is," Dyna insisted.

"But I've never done cross-country."

"You'll pick it up like that," Dyna assured her, snapping her fingers.

"Let me think about it over a cup of coffee," Maggie said. She tightened the sash on her robe and headed for the kitchen.

"That sounds like a very strenuous way of clothes shopping, too strenuous to even think about without a little fortification." *And maybe I'll come up with a much better idea in the meantime,* Maggie hoped as she scooped coffee grounds into the filter.

Unfortunately for Maggie, nothing better presented itself. Not long after calling Anne Striker and putting the best possible spin on how the book was progressing, Maggie found herself outside in the snow, braced for a morning of great exertion. She listened intently to Dyna's instructions as she stood in what seemed like very flimsy boots compared to the downhill version she was used to, on much narrower skis at the edge of the cabin's outside steps. That was the farthest she was willing to go at this point. Only the necessity of being inconspicuous at the fundraiser had pushed her to agree to this madness.

Dyna demonstrated the sliding-walking motions she would have to do, moving around the cabin's front yard with ease and tramping down tracks Maggie could use. Maggie tried it, feeling uncoordinated at first, but quickly found Dyna had been right. It was easy. At least here in the yard it was easy.

"You're getting it," Dyna said.

"I think I am," Maggie agreed, and promptly pinned one ski under the other, lost her balance, and fell down.

"You'll have to watch that," Dyna said as she helped Maggie right herself.

"I'll certainly try," Maggie said, brushing off her pants.

Dyna had told her to dress more lightly than she would for downhill skiing. "You'll work up your own heat real soon," she had promised. As Maggie followed her down Hadley Road and onto the trail in the woods, which snowmobilers had apparently already ridden through and packed down, she soon found herself lowering the zipper on her jacket to let in cool air. Minutes later she begged Dyna to stop and let her catch her breath.

"You're getting tired because you don't have a real smooth action yet. Don't worry, it'll come," Dyna promised.

In how many years, Maggie wondered. She took deep breaths and waited for her heart to slow down, then gamely followed again in Dyna's tracks. She kicked and pushed and glided as best she could, stopping less and less as they moved through the woods, and was just beginning to enjoy the effort when she realized she could see Main Street through the trees.

"It was right around here where I found Ali," Dyna said, pausing. Maggie looked where Dyna's ski pole pointed, but the only thing to see was freshly fallen snow piled around wintry brown, leafless trees.

"So the vet said he's okay?" Maggie asked, remembering the call Dyna had made to the veterinary clinic while Maggie dressed.

"Yeah, he says I can come get him as soon as the roads are clear for driving. They spoke to Leslie, and she's glad to have me take him." Dyna's eyes had narrowed as she mentioned Leslie, and Maggie knew she was still convinced Leslie had tried to dispose of poor Ali in a most unforgivable way.

Maggie didn't comment, and they pushed on to Main Street. The sidewalks had been cleared, so they stepped out of their skis and carried them over their shoulders as they walked. Maggie was glad the dress shop wasn't too far up Main. Although these skis were lighter than the downhill type, they were still an effort to lug, and she wished they had decided to leave them at the end of the path. Surely the skis wouldn't have disappeared when they went back for them, she thought. But then again, as had been dramatically made clear to her, this town wasn't always as crime-free and innocent as it seemed.

"There it is," Dyna said, pointing to the dress shop up ahead. Maggie joined Dyna in jamming her skis into the mound of snow at the curb, dusted the snow off as best she could, and followed her into the store.

Ski Lady Boutique was larger than it looked from outside, and carried a selection of women's clothing far beyond ski apparel. Dyna apparently knew her way around the store as she led the way purposefully to the rear. A woman who Maggie remembered as having spoken up at the town meeting against rezoning turned toward them, smiling. Middle-aged, elegantly coiffed, and what she herself would probably describe as a "perfect size 14," she replaced a suit she had been holding onto the rack near her and approached them.

"Hi Mona. Guess what we're here for," Dyna said.

"Since you clearly made considerable effort to get here this snowy morning, I imagine you need something to wear for the dinner tonight."

"Right! I hope you're not all sold out."

"Oh, I think we'll be able to find something you'll like. Let's see, this should be your size here, right?" Mona led Dyna to a row of brightly colored dresses, then took Maggie over to her own section, one size lower. They pawed through the racks, occasionally pulling something out and holding it up against themselves.

In the end, Dyna chose a floaty lavender dress that put roses in her cheeks. Maggie had wavered on a black dress, but finally decided to go with a green one that might get use someday for a school function. She let Mona help her choose a necklace that would elevate her outfit to the level of tonight's event. Thank goodness Dyna had discovered some basic dress shoes left behind by both her and her mother, which they could each use tonight. One less purchase to worry about.

As Mona wrapped their purchases in tissue and totaled bills, she chatted about that evening's dinner. "The whole town should be there, the adults, that is. Everyone's dying to see what the Warwicks, I mean Mrs. Warwick, will have arranged."

"I understand Dan Morgan's doing the catering," Maggie said. Her gaze had wandered back to where the black dress hung. It was still sending out a siren song that her innate practicality had managed to muffle but not completely silence.

"Yes, and he does such wonderful things with food. I hear he's even doing a vegetarian table for Regina and her friends."

Dyna's eyes lit up. "Great! Maggie picked up our tickets yesterday from Regina. We only just heard about the event, which is why we didn't have anything to wear."

Mona looked over to Maggie. "What did you think of her place?"

"It's interesting. She told me about it having been built by her grandfather."

"Yes, she's very proud of the house, and of her family. Most of it." Mona's voice had dropped to a tone of confidentiality. "I don't suppose she mentioned her brother, did she?"

"Her brother?" Maggie asked, surprised. "She told me she was the last of the line. I assumed she had no siblings."

"She doesn't, now." Mona had paused in her folding to look at Maggie and Dyna with serious eyes. "He committed suicide, years ago, as a young man."

"Oh, how awful," Dyna cried.

Maggie waited, sure that Mona planned to tell them more. She was right.

"He had been the family's black sheep, from what I hear, younger than Regina by two or three years. But where she firmly followed in the family's path of straight and narrow, as she does now, Trenton was living wild. He was what I guess they called in those days a wastrel. He was driving his parents to distraction, and Regina, I hear, hated it even worse."

Mona paused. "She was the one who found him."

"What had happened?" Maggie asked.

"Shot. He shot himself. With his father's own rifle. Regina was out walking in the woods near the pond, and said she found him there."

"Did he leave a note?"

"No note. But I'm told everyone assumed he felt he had disgraced the family enough."

Maggie pictured Regina's living room, so carefully maintained. Even her father's hunting rifles. Was the one that killed her brother there too, she wondered? Cleaned and oiled? Had Trenton actually been the one who felt that his disgraceful life had to end? Or had Regina?

Maggie shook her head to chase away those gruesome thoughts, and was glad when more customers came in, ending Mona's chronicle. She and Dyna picked up their purchases, packed now in sturdy plastic bags tied with twine, with ends they could loop over their arms backpack style, and said their good-byes.

"Gosh, what a story," Dyna said, as they retrieved their skis from the snow pile.

"Yes," Maggie agreed, struggling to hoist the skis onto her shoulder while protecting the precious cargo on her back, at the same time trying to hold onto a pair of ski poles.

As they tramped down Main Street and back to the path, Maggie wondered how similar Regina's attitude might have been towards both a disruptive brother and a disruptive businessman. Both problems in her life had been eliminated. Regina was clearly a take-charge woman, but to what extent had she taken charge in these cases?

Maggie wondered, and vowed to look into it, one way or another.

Chapter Fourteen

Leslie's house blazed with light as Maggie turned into her street that night.

"Wow! Looks like a party going on there," Dyna said.

"You might think so. Where do you suppose I should park?"

"Follow that white Blazer. It looks like Leslie's got valet parking set up."

Maggie pulled into a short line of cars. When hers reached the snow-free front walk of the Warwick house she was waved to a stop by a parka-clad teenaged boy who opened her door, helped her out, and quickly took her place in the driver's seat.

As she stood on the sidewalk with Dyna watching her car speed out of sight, Maggie swallowed the fear that she would never see it again in the same condition, then turned toward the house. "Thank goodness the snowplows cleared Hadley in time for us to get here. Let's hope most everyone else shows up too. We need to try to learn as much as we can, things that will help Elizabeth."

"Yeah, we'll pump everyone for information, while they're scarfing down goodies and off their guard."

"But discreetly," Maggie said, smiling. "Always discreetly."

As they opened the front door Maggie heard a crescendo of music coming from inside. Laughter and the tinkle of dishes and glassware filled in-between beats of the melody. Leslie stood near the door greeting guests, dressed in a very unwidowlike glittery slinky silver gown. Looking at her, Maggie's pleasure in her own new green dress slipped several notches. However, the music and a glimpse of the festive decorations within managed to keep her mood at party level.

"I'm so glad y'all came," Leslie sang out as Mrs. Hanson quickly relieved them of their coats.

"Your place looks wonderful," Maggie said. And you do too, she thought, but found she couldn't quite bring herself to say so. Maggie tried to justify this by telling herself Leslie must know how great she looked and surely was tired of hearing it, and almost succeeded. I really should try harder, she thought, to be more gracious to my murder suspects.

Glancing at Dyna, Maggie saw she wore a rather tight smile, and knew she must be thinking of Ali. His homecoming from the vet's had been postponed to tomorrow because of a small setback in his condition.

Leslie's thoughts, however, were clearly far from anything as unpleasant as the cat she so disliked as she smiled and gestured toward the living room.

"Please go on in and help yourselves to whatever you like. Dan Morgan's simply outdone himself tonight."

More guests were arriving, and Maggie and Dyna moved out of the way and into the crowded living room. A pianist sat at the baby grand angled into the corner, playing a variety of show tunes. Flowers sprouted from nearly every nook and cranny of the room, and the delicious aroma of unidentifiable delicacies floated through the air. Maggie looked at Dyna, whose expression had relaxed considerably.

"Looks like we'll get our money's worth," Maggie said.

"Just might. Are you hungry yet? I can wait a bit. I see a bar set up near the sun room. Want to start there?"

Several people greeted them as they wound their way through the crowd. Maggie saw Susan Larson and her mayor husband over near the piano, and waved as Susan looked over with a smile. Annette stood with several others at a food table in the dining room, filling a plate. She wore a puffy red dress that unfortunately accentuated her round shape.

Dyna asked the bartender for a white wine. Maggie was

tempted to do the same, but thought she'd better keep her head clear tonight and instead asked for ginger ale. "Put it in a stem glass, though, would you?" she asked, hoping it would look as though she were sipping champagne. The bartender nodded as though he got that request often.

Alexander didn't seem concerned about concealing his choice, though. As Maggie reached for her ginger ale, Alexander came up beside her and ordered a double scotch on the rocks, without the rocks. He turned to Maggie with a grin, and she managed a polite smile. She noticed Karin across the room with her back turned. Their son, thankfully, must be safely at home tonight.

Dyna had wandered over to talk to Annette, and Maggie walked over to join her.

"These appetizers are out of this world!" Annette declared, polishing off the rest of one in her hand and reaching for another.

Dan Morgan stood at the end of the table, dressed in a dark suit and looking more dinner guest than caterer. His work must be done, Maggie thought, although his gaze roamed the table, checking and re-checking the display of ham, chicken, and roast beef, as well as elaborate vegetable platters and hors d'oeuvres. He bowed his head in acceptance of Annette's praise.

"Wherever do you come up with these ideas?" she asked him. "I would love the recipe."

A nearby woman looked up eagerly at the word "recipe" and moved closer. Dan looked decidedly uncomfortable and at a loss for words when Leslie suddenly appeared and came to his rescue.

"Dan doesn't need recipes. He's a magician! That's all there is to it. An absolute magician. Isn't this table fabulous?" She took Dan's arm and pulled it through her own. Maggie saw him smile, and realized it must be the first time she saw him do so. Leslie led him away from the table. "But now it's time for him to relax and have some fun. No more shop talk for you!" she said, shaking a finger at him. Annette and the other woman watched him go with down-turned mouths, and quickly turned back to the table for consolation.

Leslie and Dan blended into the crowd, and looking after them, Maggie caught sight of Paul Dekens standing with Karin.

"I feel sorry for Elizabeth having to miss all this," she said quietly to Dyna.

"Yeah," Dyna agreed, looking in the same direction. "She could have been there, right next to Paul, if all this stuff hadn't happened."

"Well, time to start working on getting her life back the way it should be." Maggie grabbed a cracker round loaded with something green and what looked like shrimp pieces. "Shall we split up and see what we can learn?"

"Okay. Wonder where that vegetarian table's set up?" Dyna said, and wandered off toward the den.

Maggie was looking around, undecided where to go first, when she saw John Severin over near a window. She nearly didn't recognize him out of uniform, and found herself having mixed feelings at seeing him here. On the one hand, she liked him, finding him sensible and intelligent. But on the other hand, she hadn't liked his warning her away from police business at all, and feared he might be an obstacle to her goals for tonight.

As these thoughts went through her head Maggie noticed an unusual expression on John's face, and followed the direction of his gaze. He was watching Dyna as she neared the den and the look on his face definitely said "interested male." This was quite a surprise, as Maggie had never seen anything of the sort coming from him before. His manner towards Dyna had always been friendly and slightly teasing, and, lately, forbidding. Of course Dyna did look wonderful in her lavender gown. And John was off duty.

Perhaps feeling Maggie's gaze, John suddenly looked over at her. His sheriff face quickly reappeared, and Maggie thought she saw a slight narrowing of his eyes. Well, Sheriff, if you think you're going to get in the way of my learning something tonight, you're badly underestimating me. She took a sip from her ginger ale, immediately coughed as a few bubbles went down the wrong pipe, and, struggling to recover her composure, moved away with as much grace and dignity as she could muster.

She was heading toward Paul Dekens, planning to talk to both him and Karin when Vickie, Dan's hostess, stopped her with a cheerful greeting.

"Well, hello again. Don't you look nice tonight!"

"Thank you." Maggie watched as Paul walked off toward the den, and hoped Dyna might be able to catch him there. "And you too," she answered Vickie politely. "I guess the restaurant's closed?"

"Oh, yes. It's usually only closed on Mondays, so this is quite a concession for Dan, closing up an extra day. It's not exactly a day off for him, though, is it? And he's at the restaurant even on Mondays, doing the paperwork and such. I keep telling him he'll run himself ragged if he keeps that up."

"It's not easy handling your own business," Maggie said, thinking of her own family's bakery and how it had dominated their lives.

"It would have been easier for Dan if Brenda had lived. They ran a restaurant together once before, you know, but not as owners."

"Oh?"

"Uh-huh. Where was it, now. Atlantic City? Dan!" Vickie called out to Dan, who stood a few feet away with Leslie facing people Maggie didn't recognize. He turned around. "Was your last place in Atlantic City?"

Dan's scowl returned, which immediately made him look more normal to Maggie. Clearly a private person, he didn't seem to enjoy being discussed by his employee. He nodded and said "Yes," turning back at once to his group.

Maggie heard Leslie say, "Oh, Atlantic City. I lo-ove it there. One of Jack's hotels is right near the casinos and we used to . . ." Her voice was lost in a burst of song coming from the piano area. Alexander had decided to vocalize a few bars of "New York, New York."

Vickie rolled her eyes at Maggie. "He's getting started early."

"Yes. At least he seems in a good mood."

"For now."

Maggie looked around for Karin, but she seemed to have disappeared. Regina, however, had arrived, and stood near the doorway. Maggie had a lot of things she wanted to talk to her about. Before she could even think of moving in that direction, however, Susan Larson walked up with a white-haired woman in tow.

"Hello Maggie, Vickie. Maggie, I don't think you've met our school principal, Carol Martin."

"I understand you teach math," Carol began, and Maggie was effectively pinned down to a discussion of her own school and classes. Much as she would have enjoyed it on any other occasion, tonight was not one of them. Vickie excused herself and moved on, leaving Maggie wishing she could also. Common courtesy, however, kept her with Susan and Carol, all the while trying to keep her ears alert to the conversations going on around her. When Carol turned to make a comment to Susan, Maggie glanced around, looking for Regina, and saw her talking with a few of the people Maggie remembered from the restaurant. Regina managed, somehow, to be the focus of all their attention despite her diminutive size and her drab, sparrow-like attire.

Dyna emerged from the den holding a plate piled high with edibles and Maggie saw John move in her direction.

"We haven't really had much to eat yet," Susan said, "and I for one am getting hungry. Carol?"

"Yes, I believe I'd like something now. Maggie?"

"I've been nibbling. I'll catch up with you later."

Susan and Carol moved off, and Maggie quickly checked the room and spied Karin Dekens standing alone. Having already been blocked twice from her goals, Maggie hurried over before it could happen a third time. Memories of Karin on the ski slopes with Ethan came to mind as she pressed through the crowd, mixing with less pleasant ones of the scene with Alexander at the restaurant.

Karin's demeanor was as cool and composed as ever, but a smile to Maggie as she approached lightened it considerably, much as the single strand of pearls she wore lightened her sleek black dress.

"Enjoying the party?" Karin asked.

"There's certainly a lot to enjoy," Maggie said. "I hope it raises a lot of money for the school. I imagine Ethan will be starting there soon?"

The smile, while lingering on her lips, disappeared from Karin's eyes. "He'll be kindergarten age next fall."

"You might put him somewhere else?"

"It's possible." Karin took a sip from her glass and after glancing around raised her voice a notch, changing the subject. "So, since you're here tonight, the snowplows must have been busy on your road."

"Yes, they did a great job. Dyna and I had to ski out before they got there, though, to do some shopping. Paul and Alexander must be delighted with the snow because of the extra skiers it must draw."

Karin looked at Maggie for a moment before answering. "Paul, yes." She paused again. "Alexander is concerned with other things."

As if on cue, Alexander's voice could be heard, causing Maggie to turn in his direction. He stood, fresh drink in hand, with Mayor Larson, his face a bit redder than it had been a few minutes earlier.

"It's nearly a done deal," he said, loudly enough to be heard across the room. "Big Bear will be sold to the Warwick Corporation any day now. I'm flying to New York tomorrow to work out the details."

Chapter Fifteen

Maggie, shocked, looked back at Karin, who nodded, her face as impassive as ever.

"Paul and Alexander are only two of several owners of Big Bear," Karin explained. "They are the major ones, but Alexander managed to get enough minor ones, mostly distant cousins, over to his way of thinking."

Maggie didn't have to ask how Paul felt about this. One look at his rigid face across the room told her. She was almost afraid to find Regina. When she did she saw the expression Regina had worn the night of the town meeting, jaw clamped with what must be painful pressure, sparks almost flying from her eyes.

"What about the zoning change?" Maggie asked Karin.

"Alexander feels confident that will be changed. I'm not sure how he comes by that. Perhaps he thinks if the resort is sold, the town will simply give up on it."

"He might be right."

Maggie looked back in Alexander's direction and Karin excused herself and left. Where she planned to go Maggie couldn't imagine, with Alexander's statement still hanging in the air, but she disappeared from Maggie's sight quickly. Maggie, left on her own, decided to roam and eavesdrop. Discreetly.

Most comments she heard were about Alexander's announcement. People were expressing shock, dismay, delight, and resignation. An argument or two sprang up, immediately quashed by nearby spouses. Maggie saw the dress store owner, Mona, standing in her elegantly tailored evening suit some distance away. She was speaking to the gentleman with her through clenched teeth, making it unnecessary for Maggie to hear her words to guess their content.

Near the doorway to the sun room, Maggie felt a touch on her shoulder and turned to see Dyna.

"Did you hear him?" Dyna asked.

"Who didn't?"

"Yeah, he made sure of that, didn't he? It's awful, though. How can he do such a terrible thing?"

"It must benefit him financially, and I suppose that's all he cares about."

"Poor Karin. And Paul. And everyone!" Dyna grabbed the last stuffed cherry tomato on her plate, and popped it in her mouth, chewing glumly. Music drifted over from the piano, and a few couples had started dancing in the sun room, now cleared of most of its furniture and larger plants.

Maggie saw John approaching and braced herself for another warning. But she felt oddly invisible when he passed her by and asked Dyna if she would like to dance. Looking surprised but pleased, Dyna handed her empty plate to Maggie and took John's hand to be led near the other dancers.

Maggie watched them for a while, happy to see Dyna perk up and amused to see John trying, somewhat unsuccessfully, to keep time to the music. Her thoughts drifted to Rob, remembering the last time they had danced together, and she felt a stab of melancholy. Their promise to call every night had been quickly disintegrating. Tonight, she promised herself, when she got home, she would . . . Her reverie was interrupted by the sound of Leslie's voice.

"I can't eat yet," Leslie insisted. "I haven't had a thing to drink. I'm parched!"

"Let me get you some water then," Dan answered her.

"Water?"

Maggie turned to see Dan firmly turning Leslie away from

the bar. "Alcohol dulls the palate. Are you going to let all the work I did go to waste by not tasting it properly?"

Leslie looked a bit uncertain, then smiled and shook her head. "Of course not." She let herself be led away from the bar as Dan explained the choices on the table.

Maggie turned and saw Vickie watching the same scene. She smiled at Maggie and walked over.

"I just realized," Maggie said, "that I haven't seen Leslie holding a drink so far this evening."

"That might be Dan's influence. He detests hard liquor, and only offers wine at the restaurant because of customer demand."

"Is that because of what he just said? That it dulls the palate?"

"I'm not sure. I only know that he never drinks, and Brenda didn't either. But then, she was always watching her weight, and called alcohol empty calories."

"Speaking of empty calories . . ." Maggie nodded towards Alexander, who had loosened a too-tight tie and shirt collar, and was draining the last of his latest drink. His eyes had taken on a glaze, and he looked around with some confusion as if he had forgotten for the moment where he was. Spotting Dan and Leslie near the food table, he suddenly lurched in their direction, bumping against an elderly woman who had to be caught and balanced by her husband. Alexander moved on without apology, earning a look of disgust from several bystanders.

"Hey, got anything to eat here that won't kill me?" he said loudly as he approached the table.

Leslie's head jerked up, and Dan scowled, putting an arm around her shoulder.

"I mean, I don't like a lot of extra seasoning." Alexander picked up a carrot stick and looked at the dip near it. "I hear too many people have funny plants around. You didn't sprinkle any of them in this, did you, Leslie?" Alexander poked his finger into the creamy dip and pulled it out, looking at it with mock serious scrutiny.

Dan stepped between Alexander and Leslie, moving her

back. "Mrs. Warwick had nothing to do with the food preparation."

"Mrs. Warwick? Oh, yeah, the grieving widow. Or maybe I should say the merry widow. You two gettin' along pretty well, huh? The widower and the widow. Just think. If you hadn't come here from Atlantic City you two might never have met. Right? But then, maybe if you'd stayed there, Brenda'd still be around."

Maggie heard a gasp from someone nearby. Suddenly Paul appeared, grabbing his brother's arm and speaking in a low, angry voice. Maggie couldn't hear it all, but the words "jerk" and "think of Karin" came through.

"But brother dear, it's Karin I'm thinking of. She must be heartbroken to see ol' Dan here moving in on someone else. You should know how that feels, watching Jack and Elizabeth . . ."

Paul's fist would have connected with Alexander's face if John hadn't moved quickly, grabbing it from behind. John immediately moved between them, facing Paul and firmly pushing him back.

"It's not worth it, Paul. Just let me get him out of here. Go on over to the den and cool down. Let's not let him ruin the whole party."

John continued talking to Paul in a calm, steady voice, until Paul turned and walked away. John then took Alexander firmly by the arm and over his drunken protests marched him to the kitchen, and, Maggie assumed, out the back door.

Maggie moved towards the foyer and saw Paul helping Karin with her coat, and could only imagine the emotions coursing through each. It seemed, however, that only the guests closest to the unfortunate incident were aware of it, as lively chatter continued in the farther reaches of the party. Maggie had no doubt, though, that the details of it would soon spread, perhaps with a few extra added in for good measure. With that thought she looked around for Annette. She was jabbering animatedly, with many significant looks toward the front door as Paul and Karin departed.

Maggie was glad the noise level of the crowd was such that

Karin wouldn't have heard most of what was being said. She was probably acutely aware of it anyway, as on other occasions, which likely accounted for her usual air of cool detachment. Maggie wondered what really went on inside Karin's head, and what her next move after this latest humiliation would be.

She was standing alone, thinking, when Regina passed by and read her mind.

"Pity, isn't it?" Regina said.

When Maggie nodded, Regina looked away and added in a quieter tone, as though to herself, "Some people the world would be a lot better off without."

Alexander's embarrassing outburst didn't break up the party. There was still plenty of food left to consume, drinks to drink, and gossip to relish. But Maggie, in her continued roaming, was learning little more than that most of the townspeople had had a low opinion of Alexander for quite some time, and weren't too surprised at how he'd acted. Since they were in Leslie's home, they generally avoided comment on what he had said regarding her, and confined their remarks to Alexander's drinking problem, his gambling problem, and his quite likely marriage problem.

Elizabeth's name was brought up a few times, though, and to Maggie's dismay it seemed to be generally assumed that Elizabeth would soon be charged with Jack Warwick's murder. If anyone felt differently, they were keeping silent, and since Maggie's aim was only to overhear, she had to bite her tongue more than once to keep from defending her friend. It was depressing to learn that so many of Elizabeth's neighbors were finding it that easy to believe in her guilt.

Maggie looked around more than once for Regina, hoping to get a few minutes' conversation with her. But after that disconcerting comment she had made after Alexander's exit, Regina seemed to have disappeared into thin air, and Maggie's frustration grew.

When guests began drifting to the foyer to leave, Maggie gave up. There was nothing more she could accomplish. Since she hadn't had much to eat the whole evening, she grabbed a few quick bites then joined Dyna in asking for their coats.

Outside, as they waited for her car, Maggie shivered from the cold.

"It must have dropped twenty degrees since we came," she complained, shifting her weight from one foot to another in her thin-soled pumps, hands jammed in her pockets and shoulders hunched against the cold blowing wind.

"Here comes your car."

Maggie climbed in and waited for Dyna to buckle up. She made a U-turn and headed home, waiting for the heater to raise the temperature at least a few degrees. Her breath puffing visibly as she talked, Maggie shared what little she had learned.

"Did you do any better?" she asked Dyna.

Dyna admitted she hadn't, her snooping activities having been largely diverted by John. Maggie's mood slumped further.

They arrived home, and as soon as she stepped inside Dyna pulled her shoes off. "I'm exhausted. I think I'll just go to bed."

"Don't you want to have some tea? Talk a while?" Maggie asked, not feeling ready for bed herself. She hoped Dyna would stay up with her, chase away some of the gloom she felt descending.

Dyna, however, seemed ready for pleasant dreams. She shook her head with a sleepy smile. "I can hardly keep my eyes open. See you in the morning."

Maggie watched Dyna disappear up the wrought-iron steps. She wandered into the kitchen, feeling physically tired but mentally keyed up, the evening's events running through her mind. She wasn't sure she had learned anything that would be in any way helpful to Elizabeth, and that, along with the encroaching fatigue, depressed her.

She remembered her plan to call Rob and picked up the phone. Talking to him would help. It had been too long. She wanted to feel his hug reaching through the line. She needed him to tell her that she was doing okay, that all would be well.

What she got was, "This is Rob. I'm sorry I'm not here right now. If you leave a message after . . ."

Maggie hung up without leaving a message. She walked over to the sliding glass door and gazed out at the darkness, which seemed endless and empty. Maggie leaned her head against the glass, feeling its chill against her skin.

Was she doing any good at all, she wondered? Was Elizabeth any better off now than she was three days ago? Maggie sighed. She just didn't know.

Chapter Sixteen

Maggie dragged herself out of bed the next day. Somewhere in the middle of the night her brain had finally stopped tossing around its store of conflicting thoughts and allowed her to have a few hours of sleep. She stumbled down the steps to find Dyna seated at the kitchen counter, sipping her tea.

Dyna looked up. "Wow, if I didn't know better, I'd think you were hungover. Was that really just ginger ale you sipped all night?"

Maggie smiled. "I had a rough night. Just give me a minute."

Maggie poured out coffee, grateful that Dyna had brewed a pot. She held the mug between both hands, and, sipping slowly, wandered over to the sliding glass door. The day outside looked grey and cold. A blue jay flitted from tree to deck and back again. Its squawkings seemed to be aimed directly at Maggie. She gave a sigh and turned away from the window.

"Dyna, I'm worried we're not getting anywhere. I had hoped to make much more progress than we did last night. It seems like this whole thing is just going in circles."

"It's not all that bad," Dyna said. She stood up and bustled into the small kitchen. "You're probably just having a blood-sugar low. You didn't eat much last night, did you? I was just thinking it'd be fun to make pancakes. I haven't made them in ages, and we've got all the stuff right here. I'll even fry a little bacon for you to go with it. How's that sound?"

127

"It sounds like my mother," Maggie said, smiling. "No problem is so bad it can't be fixed with good food."

"Sure doesn't hurt. You go up and get dressed, and I'll call you when it's ready. We can talk more afterwards."

Dyna began pulling bowls and pans out of the cupboard with so much clatter and enthusiasm that Maggie couldn't argue. She carried her coffee upstairs with her, feeling her mood lift a bit with each step. By the time she had dried off from her shower and dressed, she could smell the tantalizing aroma of cooked bacon. She grabbed her socks, pulled them on, and hurried down to the kitchen.

Maggie did justice to Dyna's pancakes, mopping up the last of the syrup on her plate with her final forkful.

"Where'd you learn to make these?" she asked, as Dyna watched with the satisfaction of a doting grandmother.

"Oh, we used to make pancakes every weekend. Sometimes waffles. Dad liked to make them, and he'd try different kinds, potato, blueberry, whatever. I guess I caught the bug. Or inherited the pancake gene, or something."

"You picked a good one to inherit."

"Yeah, but I sure picked the wrong gene for noses. Mom has this little turned-up nose, and Dad has the one with the bump in it. You see which one I got."

"Your nose is fine. And John seemed to think so too, last night."

Dyna's cheeks on each side of her fine/bumpy nose turned pink, which made Maggie smile.

"He was probably just being nice."

"John doesn't strike me as someone who is nice without the right feeling behind it."

Dyna smiled. "Yeah, maybe. He's a pretty up-front kinda guy. And he can be fun when he wants to. We were having a good time. At least we were until Alexander ended it all."

"Alexander spoiled a good time for a lot of people last night." Maggie remembered Paul escorting Karin out in a hurry, as well as the dismay Alexander's announcement had brought to many.

"He said he was flying to New York today. I hope he has one doozy of a hangover to spoil his day. He deserves it."

Maggie picked up the dishes and carried them to the dishwasher. She ran hot water and soap into the sink and began washing up the skillet.

"I have the feeling," she said as she scrubbed at crusted grease with a soapy sponge, "that Alexander's life is one long headache. He's not a happy man."

"No, but, you know, he should be. I mean, he's got a great wife, and a terrific little boy. And look what he does. It's like," Dyna thought for a moment, "like someone who has a fantastic dinner in front of him and then ruins it with catsup or hot sauce."

"Mmm." Maggie looked around for a wire scrubber, found it, and went back to work on the skillet. "Mentioning food reminds me that Alexander certainly seems to have something against Dan Morgan. I wonder if it's because he sees how Dan is able to appreciate what he himself has been so careless with."

"You don't think Karin and Dan are involved with each other, do you?"

"I don't know. Maybe just to the extent that Dan treats Karin like an intelligent, talented person and she responds to that."

"I didn't see them anywhere near each other last night."

"No, Dan stayed mainly with Leslie. Which was interesting."

Maggie rinsed and wiped the skillet, then turned on the dishwasher. As it started chugging she left the kitchen and sat in one of the blue tweed chairs.

"I spoke with Karin a bit. She was as reserved as usual, but she was definitely unhappy with Alexander's push to sell Big Bear."

"Yeah, she's gotta be."

"Does she have any family here? Other than Alexander and Paul, I mean."

"Gee, I don't think so. Why?"

"I guess I was just wondering if she might choose to stay here."

"You mean without Alexander?"

"If she has to. Do you see her wanting to eagerly go wherever he decides to go?"

"Not the way he's been acting lately." Dyna moved to the floor and assumed the lotus position, tucking her legs and feet into what looked to Maggie more like the "pretzel" position. "But if he sells Big Bear," Dyna continued, "Cedar Hill will change. Karin might not want to stay in the new Cedar Hill."

"Mmm. And Regina won't like the changes that are bound to come either."

"That's for sure."

The phone rang. Dyna looked too tangled up to move quickly, so Maggie went to pick it up.

"Hello?"

"Maggie, it's John Severin."

"Oh, hi, John." Maggie looked over at Dyna with a smile. Dyna's face had lit up at hearing John's name.

"Is Dyna there with you?"

"Yes, shall I put her on?"

"No, not now. I'm just calling to tell you both to stay put."

"Why?" Maggie asked, suddenly uneasy. John had spoken brusquely. He was definitely calling as 'Sheriff John,' not as friend John.

"Lock your doors, and don't go out until I can come by."

"John, what's wrong. What happened?"

Maggie heard John take a deep breath. He clearly didn't like having to say what came next. "Alexander Dekens was found dead early this morning. Killed by a rifle shot, as he was driving to catch his plane."

Chapter Seventeen

The cabin's interior light, already grey from the sunless day, had become leaden with the news of Alexander's death. Maggie switched on lamps in the downstairs living area, which brightened the room but did little to relieve the gloom. She opened her laptop, then snapped it shut. She knew she couldn't concentrate on math puzzles right now.

Maggie reflected on how different she felt hearing about Alexander's death from when she had heard about Jack Warwick. Jack's death by poisoning had been a shock, but she had known, and, truthfully, cared, little about him at the time. She had listened to Jack speak, but hadn't spoken to him.

Alexander, on the other hand, had become quite familiar. Maggie hadn't grown to like him, but he was little Ethan's father, Paul's brother, and the man whom Karin had loved enough, once upon a time, to marry.

Now he was dead. Shot. But by whom, Maggie was unable yet to wonder, as she was still working on the simple realization that it had happened.

Dyna, apparently, had the same problem. She wandered aimlessly from room to room, window to window, saying little but looking stunned.

"Maybe you'd like to work on your yoga while we're waiting," Maggie suggested.

Dyna looked over. "Yeah, maybe." But she made no move

to do so, instead wandering into the kitchen to fold and re-fold the dish towel.

The phone rang. Maggie, who was nearest, picked it up.

"This is Carrie, from Dr. Fortier's office." Maggie knew from the tone of her voice that the veterinarian's receptionist hadn't heart about Alexander. "Ali is doing well and is ready to be picked up. Would you like to come this afternoon?"

"I'll have to get back to you on that, Carrie. Today might be difficult."

"We don't mind keeping him, but he's full of energy and raring to go. We're open 'till five. Just let us know and we'll have him ready."

Maggie promised to call, and hung up. "Ali's ready to be picked up," she said to Dyna.

"I forgot all about him! I still have to get a litter box and food and all."

"We can get everything easily. I'm sure John will give us the go-ahead very soon." Having said that, Maggie walked to the glass door and gazed out at the road, willing his sheriff's car to come driving up the hill. Maggie thought of Elizabeth, wondering if she should call her. Better wait until I have more information, she decided.

Another thought came to her on the heels of that one, more hopeful than the last. Had Alexander been shot by the same person who murdered Jack Warwick? If so, that would surely clear Elizabeth! It hardly seemed likely that Elizabeth would own a rifle or even know how to fire one. That could and would be easily verified. John would have to look for someone who did.

Maggie opened her mouth to share this encouraging thought with Dyna when movement on the road caught her eye—John's car!

"Here he comes," she called out, and Dyna slipped off the kitchen counter stool and hurried over to the window. Dyna watched as the sheriff's car pulled into the cabin's driveway, then hurried to open the side door.

Maggie heard John tramp up the outer steps, and tap the snow off his boots.

"He's really dead?" Maggie heard Dyna ask. John must have nodded, for as he stepped into the small foyer, Dyna leaned against him. He put his arms around her and held her for a moment, then let go and pulled off his cap. Dyna led him into the living room.

"Coffee?" she asked, her face somber. "Something to eat?"

"No, I can't stay but a minute. We're trying to get around, check that everyone's all right."

"What exactly happened?" Maggie asked.

"All we know right now, and what we've already told the papers, is that Alexander was apparently on his way to Boston to catch a shuttle for New York. He left his house about five-thirty this morning. He hadn't gone very far out of town, hadn't reached the main highway. An early morning hiker came upon his car in a ditch off Evergreen Road. He called it in as an accident. The paramedics discovered he had been shot in the head."

"Definitely murder?"

"We're treating it as such, although it could have been a hunter's stray bullet. It's small game season right now."

"If it was murder," Maggie said, "someone was a very good shot to aim accurately at a moving target."

John looked at her, not commenting.

"Would you say Alexander's death is connected to Jack Warwick's?"

"You're beginning to sound like one of those newspaper reporters."

"I'm sorry, I don't mean to badger you, John. I'm only thinking of Elizabeth. If the same person killed Alexander as killed Jack, it must be obvious that person is not Elizabeth."

"We're a long way from any conclusions."

"But Maggie's right, isn't she?" Dyna jumped in. "Surely you must see that Elizabeth was set up with that evidence you found. That she couldn't hurt a fly."

"I thought we agreed last night we wouldn't get into any of that."

"Yes, but John—"

"John's right," Maggie interrupted Dyna. John clearly

wasn't about to discuss or admit anything about the ongoing investigations. No use making him angry with Dyna.

"I'd like to check your locks, if you don't mind," John said. He had become Sheriff John once more. "And ask you to be extremely cautious." John went to the sliding glass door, clicking the lock off and on, testing the door. He glanced at a security bar standing upright in the door's track.

"Best keep this in place," he said, flipping it down. "You won't need to go out onto your deck in this weather."

He walked around, checking the cabin's windows. "Don't go walking outdoors alone for the time being. If you need to go out, head for populated areas. Don't open your door to strangers."

"I don't think it's a stranger we have to worry about, do you?" Maggie asked.

John glanced up the stairs, walked past them, and put his hat back on. "Keep your doors locked at all times."

"But John, who would want to harm us?" Dyna asked.

John's eyes softened for a moment as he looked at Dyna. "No one, I hope. I'm just asking you to be careful. Be aware."

"We will," Maggie promised.

After John left, Maggie tried shifting Dyna's thoughts to lighter matters, suggesting they get what she needed now for Ali.

"John won't disapprove of us going out together to the busy part of town. I've never had a cat, Dyna. Do they need cat beds, special equipment?"

"Missy liked people beds. I think cats pretty much make their own decisions on that. I don't know what to get. Let's just go to a pet store and look around."

They were gathering up keys and jackets when the phone rang. It was Carrie, calling from the veterinary office again.

"I forgot to tell you that Mrs. Hanson, the lady who works for Mrs. Warwick, dropped off a few things for Ali. There's a carrier, litter box, bowls, and some other things."

"That's great Carrie. Thanks."

When Maggie told Dyna, though, she wrinkled her nose.

"Maybe I'll use the carrier, but I don't want the other stuff. I want Ali to make a fresh start. I want him to feel safe."

"You'll let all the things from Leslie go to waste?" Maggie asked. Her innate frugality cringed at replacing what didn't need to be replaced.

"Maybe they can use it at the vet's. I don't want it."

Dyna said it with such firmness that Maggie let it go. If spending a few dollars on new equipment for Ali made her happy, Maggie was all for it.

The "few dollars," however, rapidly escalated as Dyna roamed through the pet store. She had already chosen the basics, and began piling cat toys, brushes, and cat treats into her basket. Maggie finally spoke up when Dyna stopped to check out a "cat condo," a four-foot-high maze of carpet-covered perches, hideaways, and scratching posts.

"Remember, you've got to take this home with you eventually. On a plane."

"I know, but you've got your car. I thought . . ."

Dyna stopped after a quick glance at Maggie. Maggie wasn't thrilled at having the cat move in with them, but could hardly object since, after all, it was Dyna's cabin. Her own car, though, was under her complete control, and lugging a fur-loaded cat contraption back to Baltimore among her luggage and laptop was not going to happen. No way.

"I guess I have enough for now," Dyna said, and turned the basket toward the check-out.

They were loading it all in Dyna's car when Maggie suggested they stop at Elizabeth's before picking up Ali.

"I want to talk to her about what's happened. Just a few minutes."

"Sure. There's plenty of time to get Ali. I'd like to see Liz too."

After the short drive up Main, Dyna parked next to the snow-piled curb in front of the Book Nook. The store's windows were dark.

"I really wish she'd open for business," Dyna said. "It must be too depressing to sit all alone back there. Course she's got plenty to read."

They climbed out of the car, and Maggie led Dyna around to the back door. A light tap brought Elizabeth to the window, and seeing them, she quickly unlocked the door and opened it. She seemed in better shape than the last time Maggie had been there. No afghan clutched around her this time, and the television, instead of being blank, was tuned to a talk show whose subject, judging from occasional laughter, was cheerful. She had obviously taken some pains with her hair—always a good sign. It looked freshly shampooed and curled softly on her neck. Her smile, however, did not reach her eyes.

"You've heard what happened this morning?" Maggie asked.

"Yes, one of the deputies came by. He checked my doors and windows and warned me to keep them locked, but I think he was also looking around for a stash of rifles and ammunition. He asked if I'd been out early today."

"As if you could ever do such a thing!" Dyna's face was indignant.

"I don't blame them."

"But, Liz, Maggie thinks this could actually prove your innocence, in Jack's murder, I mean."

Elizabeth looked at Maggie, who nodded.

"I think the two deaths could be related. If the same person who poisoned Jack also shot Alexander, you would be eliminated as a suspect for not being able to have shot Alexander. You don't own a gun or know how to shoot, do you?"

"No! That would be the last thing in the world I would ever want to learn. Even for protection."

Elizabeth clicked off the television, then sank down onto the overstuffed chair. She put her hands to her face, elbows on knees. Instead of looking pleased at the possibility of being cleared she seemed more upset. Her face grew flushed.

"Oh, this is awful."

"What's wrong?" Dyna asked.

"Paul hunts." Elizabeth looked at Maggie, letting those two words hang in the air.

Maggie nodded, knowing what was going through Elizabeth's mind. Paul has guns. Paul loves Big Bear. Jack Warwick wanted to take Big Bear from him and died. Alexander wanted to dispose of Big Bear and had been shot.

"But Alexander is his brother. He couldn't . . ." Dyna stopped, unable to finish.

"I'm sure John will be questioning Paul. He'll have to. But I wouldn't worry about him yet. He might have a very good alibi. Besides, I'm sure he's not the only one in Cedar Hill with hunting rifles." As she said it, Maggie's thoughts flashed to Regina's living room. The living room with a gun case. It stood there carefully preserved, protected, polished. Had Regina learned to shoot as a young girl, Maggie wondered, at her beloved father's side, before her own strong opinions against hunting had developed?

Mona's tale at the dress shop of Regina's brother's death by gunshot ran through Maggie's mind. It was followed soon by the image of Regina at last night's dinner, coming up to Maggie after Alexander's drunken outburst. Regina, quiet and grim, had spoken in a low voice, as though thinking aloud.

"Some people the world would be better off without."

Maggie shivered.

Chapter Eighteen

"**A**li!"

Maggie rushed to prevent the large orange cat from scattering the carefully sorted papers next to her laptop.

"He's just exploring," Dyna said.

Maggie lifted the cat, probably weighing a good eighteen pounds, off the round oak table and handed him to Dyna.

"Please tell him to explore at floor level."

Dyna fell back onto one of the soft chairs, holding onto Ali, who immediately made himself comfortable on her lap. A purr that sounded to Maggie like something between asthmatic wheezing and her father's weed whacker began to emanate from the cat.

Dyna hugged the furry, vibrating creature and scratched under his chin.

"Poor little thing. He has to get used to another strange place. I wonder how many times he's had to do that."

If his other homes were with people who expected a cat to respect their possessions, probably quite a few, Maggie thought. Ali had already been removed from the food-covered kitchen counter twice, and had nearly pulled down the small lamp on Dyna's bedside table by its cord. Maggie would put up with Ali for Dyna's sake. And keep her bedroom door firmly closed at all times.

The phone rang. Since Dyna was out of reach and pinned down by the heavy feline on her lap, Maggie picked it up.

"Hey, Maggie." Her brother Joe's hearty voice rolled out. "Your friend up there still need that lawyer?"

"What?" As soon as she said it Maggie remembered asking Joe to check on the lawyer Paul was getting for Elizabeth. It was hard to believe that was only two days ago with all that had happened.

"Judd Ambler. Remember? I thought it was important."

"It is. Or it was. It's beginning to look like she won't really need him."

"Well that's good. Dave Schmidt, the lawyer I worked for last summer, says Ambler's fine, but that he's into criminal law. I thought your friend was just being sued or something."

Maggie sat down, holding the phone. She watched Dyna slide Ali off her lap with some difficulty and onto one side of the wide chair cushion. Ali had clearly decided he preferred to remain prone and wasn't helping in the least now that Dyna wanted to stand up.

Maggie hesitated, then decided to come clean. "No, she wasn't being sued." Maggie crossed her legs and braced for what she knew would come. "She was under suspicion of murder."

"What!"

"It's Elizabeth Kerr." Maggie spoke rapidly. "Betsy Kerr. I knew her from Girl Scout camp back in sixth grade. Remember that year I went to Camp Kittiwake and I came home with—"

"No, I don't remember. You're friends with a woman who murdered someone?"

"Of course not. Elizabeth didn't murder anyone. And that's why she needed a good lawyer. I was simply making sure of that."

"And what else have you been making sure of?" Joe's tone had become stern. Although younger than Maggie by two years, he had the irritating tendency to occasionally treat her as the younger sibling.

"Only that justice is done."

"Maggie . . ."

"Never mind, Joe. I already know everything you're going to say. I am being careful, and I do have to do this."

"You went up there to write a book."

"I'm doing that too." Maggie's conscience tweaked her as she said that. She knew she had hardly touched her notes lately. "Kind of," she added, recalling her intention of honesty.

Joe grunted and groused some more, and the call ended on an unsatisfactory note for both. Maggie had managed to pull a reluctant promise from him not to bother their parents with what she had told him. For now. She couldn't count on that for very long, she knew, if Joe decided he needed back-up pressure to bring her home. But surely this would all be resolved before too long. It had to be.

As Maggie hung up the phone, she stared at it a moment, thinking, then turned dolefully toward her math papers.

"What's the matter?" Dyna asked.

"Oh, Joe's giving me a hard time as usual. But he made me realize how little I've been getting done on the book. I had been toying with the idea of us taking a quick trip down to Atlantic City and I don't—"

"Atlantic City? What for?"

"To look into Alexander's activities. Alexander did much of his gambling there. I thought perhaps talking to people who had some connection with him there might turn something up, or at least give us a better picture of him."

Dyna thought for a moment. "Yeah, Annette did say he was there a lot. Gosh, what if he had some kind of secret life going on, besides the gambling, I mean. You know, like, maybe he had a mistress stashed there, and her brother was in the mob. And the brother found out he's really married and came here and shot him." Dyna frowned. "Except that wouldn't explain Jack Warwick's murder, would it?

"No, but maybe just learning where Alexander spent his time and with whom would turn up something useful."

"Yeah, I think you're right. Well, here's an idea. Why don't you stay here and I go myself? That way you can work on your book, but still keep tabs on things here."

"Hmm, that's a thought."

"Sure." Dyna was revving up now. "I could call my friend Pam. Remember, I told you about going to her housewarming once and getting so lost on the drive home? Anyway, she's in the south Jersey area, not too far from Atlantic City. She said once that lots of her neighbors work there, at the casinos and such. I could start by talking to some of them. They might have good contacts."

Maggie smiled. "That sounds like it might work."

"Sure it will. I'll just call Pam and . . . Oh!" Dyna's face fell. "But you'd be here alone. Maybe that's not such a good idea."

"Now don't you start sounding like Joe," Maggie said, shaking her head. "I can take care of myself. I've been living on my own for what—three years now?—in Baltimore, and I've picked up a thing or two about personal safety. I'll be fine. But I just thought of something else—what about you and John? Do you mind taking off just as things were starting to, well, warm up?"

"Oh, John." Dyna smiled. "He won't have time to give me a passing thought for a while. I'll just put him on hold, and we can pick up where we left off when this is all over."

Dyna headed for the steps. "Well, if you're sure about staying here by yourself, I'll give Pam a call. I've got her number in my room somewhere." She patted Ali's head as she went by. "At least you'll have Ali for company. Wasn't it lucky we picked him up today?"

Maggie looked at the huge feline, now stretched over the entire chair cushion and snoring noisily. She wasn't sure she would use the word "lucky." In fact, she had forgotten about Ali when she first considered going off with Dyna to Atlantic City. They certainly couldn't have taken him with them, and would have had to deal with arrangements for his care. Now it looked like responsibility for his care and feeding, as well as protecting most of the breakable objects of the cabin had fallen onto her. What "luck."

Maggie headed for her laptop and skirted his chair widely on her way.

Chapter Nineteen

The cabin seemed unnaturally quiet to Maggie after Dyna left. Ali had immediately commandeered Dyna's bed and lay there in the jumble of its covers, blissfully asleep, leaving Maggie to fend for herself. She didn't mind in the least and was glad of the distraction-free time to work at her computer.

As hard as she tried to concentrate on her book, though, she found her mind flitting back and forth between the mathematical problems in her notes and the very real problems surrounding her life in Cedar Hill. Never before had she had so much trouble concentrating on numbers. Only the threat of another call from her editor kept her plodding along.

When the afternoon shadows began to darken the room, Maggie got up to stretch, thinking she might heat up a quick dinner and then get back to work. She was poking through the meager pickings of the refrigerator when the phone rang.

"Maggie?" a lilting female voice asked. "This is Leslie Warwick. I'm so lonely here I could die. Will you and Dyna do me the greatest favor and come have dinner with me? It's Mrs. Hanson's day off, but there's so much left over from last night's party we could have ourselves a banquet."

Maggie thought rapidly. Dyna, she knew, considered Leslie a prime suspect and would tell Maggie in an instant not to go. She could almost hear Dyna's voice: "She poisoned her husband, as well as her cat. Go there alone, and she'll poison you too. Don't do it!"

However, though Maggie had certainly once considered Leslie a possibility in Jack's death, she was now far less certain of that than Dyna. Leslie may have had a good motive to get rid of Jack, but why poison him? A good divorce lawyer could surely have arranged a settlement that would take care of her for life. Why put herself at risk for prison or worse? And if Leslie had suddenly become enraged enough to override good sense, poison would not have been the method of choice. Something fast, like a gun, was the weapon one used in the heat of passion. Poison took time and a cool hand.

"Dyna's gone off for a couple days," Maggie said, "but I'd love to come."

"Wonderful. Come as you are," Leslie instructed. "And soon."

Maggie smiled as she hung up. She had a good supper to look forward to and an interesting evening ahead. Who knew what conversation with Leslie would turn up? Maggie fairly bounded up the stairs to get herself ready.

Leslie's home looked none the worse for wear to Maggie after last night's big party. Maggie imagined a team of house cleaners whisking away all traces of the festivities. Probably the same team had prepared the rooms beforehand as well, she mused, polishing and rearranging furniture. Then Dan Morgan had shown up with the food, cooked and ready to serve. All Leslie had to do, she guessed, was make herself beautiful, and she probably had some help with that too. Must be nice, Maggie thought. Except for what it may have cost Leslie to attain this kind of lifestyle. Sometimes the good life came with a very high price tag.

Leslie led Maggie to the kitchen, where she pulled the door of the oversized refrigerator open wide.

"See how much there is! And we even sent scads of it over to the homeless shelter in Chesterton. Those people will be eatin' like kings tonight." She started pulling out plastic containers, and Maggie pitched in, lining them up on the large kitchen table.

"Let's just open everything up," Leslie suggested, "and pick and choose whatever we want onto our plates. If something looks like it should be warmed up, the microwave is over there."

"This is great," Maggie said. "I really didn't get to try as much as I would have liked last night. Too busy talking, I guess." *Or too busy snooping.*

"I ate like a pig. After tonight, I'm going to tell Mrs. Hanson to take most of this away. My figure will be ruined." Leslie pulled a three-quarters full bottle of wine from the bottom shelf of the refrigerator and squinted at the label. "Let's see. Chablis? Or do you like red?"

"White's good." Maggie licked her fingers after putting one of Dan's salmon roe and cream cheese pastries on her plate. She looked up and saw Leslie pouring wine into only one glass, which she then held out to Maggie. She filled a glass with ice water for herself. Maggie made no comment, but remembered how Dan had steered Leslie away from alcohol during the party. It seemed to be having a lasting effect.

Leslie looked more relaxed tonight than Maggie had ever seen her. Of course last night, as hostess, she had been keyed up. But the other times, both before and after Jack's death, Leslie had demonstrated a tension that seemed of long duration. Like someone with a chronic pain who has learned to live with it. Leslie's pain, whatever its source, seemed relieved, at least for now.

When both their plates were fully loaded, Leslie directed Maggie to a small sitting area, divided from the kitchen by a built-in planter. The combination breakfast nook/family room had a stone-faced fireplace. Leslie aimed a remote control at the hearth and flames leaped up in an instant.

"There, that makes it all nice and cozy," she said. She sat on the loveseat and tucked her feet up under her.

Maggie set her wine glass on a small end table and sat across from Leslie in the only other chair, angled slightly toward the fireplace. "That's nice. Wish we had one of those," she said, nodding toward the remote. "There's a fireplace at the cabin, but the kind that actually burns wood and needs kindling and matches and such, so we haven't gotten around to using it yet." She took a sip of wine, then studied her plate, deciding where to begin.

"We could pop in a movie if you like," Leslie said. "There's boxes of them, maybe even some I've never seen."

"No, that's all right. I'd rather just talk."

"Okie-doke. You know, I just realized I hardly know anything about you. Why don't you tell me all about yourself."

Maggie rolled her eyes. "Not that much to tell." She took a bite of honey-sweet, melt-in-your-mouth ham and gave Leslie a condensed version of her life growing up in Baltimore with Joe and their parents.

Leslie had been smiling as she listened, but Maggie caught a glimpse of wistfulness in her eyes. "You're lucky," Leslie said. "I bet you've got grandparents, and aunts and uncles and all that too."

"Well, yes. Some of each. And a few cousins."

"I don't have anyone."

Leslie said it very matter-of-factly, and Maggie was stopped cold.

"You mean, no family whatsoever?"

"No family, nothing. Mama died before I finished high school. Never had a daddy. No husband now, either. Although, I didn't really *have* him for quite a while."

Maggie said nothing, and Leslie continued.

"I knew about his affair with Elizabeth, you know. But I also knew about the affairs before that." She reached for her water glass and took a swallow, looking up after a moment with a bright smile. "But I asked about you, and here I am talkin' about me. Just ignore me and go on."

"Let's see. What else," Maggie said. "Oh, I managed to get through college, and have been teaching high school math ever since, and loving it."

Leslie looked at Maggie. "You must be very smart."

Maggie laughed, shaking her head, and popped a marinated mushroom in her mouth.

"You are," Leslie insisted. "Smart women don't mess up their lives like I have."

"I guess it helps to have someone watching out for you," Maggie said, softly.

"Uh-huh."

The phone rang, and Leslie stood up to answer it.

"Oh, Dan, hi," she said, and wandered a few steps into the kitchen, receiver to her ear. Maggie played the part of the good guest, absorbed in her food and pretending not to hear a word of a conversation that had nothing to do with her. But in fact there was little to hear. Dan, it seemed, did most of the talking. Leslie finally did murmur a few words at the end, but her back was to Maggie, who could decipher none of it.

Leslie ended the call and returned to her chair.

"Dan's so sweet," she said as she took her plate back onto her lap. "He offered to come over with some of his fabulous wild mushroom soup. He knows how I love it. But I told him we still had enough leftovers to feed an army."

"Maybe he should take the soup over to Karin."

"Hmm? Oh. Yes. Perhaps he will." Leslie looked doubtful. Whether it was over the possibility of Dan's taking something to Karin, or over how she would feel if he did, Maggie couldn't tell.

Maggie felt a surge of protectiveness for the woman across from her. A wellspring of sisterly, motherly, grandmotherly advice, the kind Leslie may never actually have been given, bubbled up. "Leslie, do you know anything about Dan, other than that he's a restaurant owner?"

"Dan? Well, no, I guess not. I do know he's a widower." Leslie offered that extra bit of information proudly, as though to prove she wasn't totally in the dark.

"Did you know him when he was in Atlantic City? I think you said something about Jack having a hotel there."

"No. I never met Dan until we came here. Why?"

Maggie hesitated. "It's just, well, it's probably not a good idea, right now, for you to jump into anything. I mean, you've had it pretty rough, emotionally, for a while, and maybe you need to take some time out. Just to get yourself together. Don't you think?"

Leslie stared at Maggie, who waited, not sure what kind of reaction was coming.

"Was I getting into something?" Leslie asked.

"It looked like you might be."

Leslie stared some more, and Maggie could almost see the wheels and cogs of her mind working. They might have been a little rusty, but they still worked. "I think you're right. I didn't realize it, but it was awfully nice to have a man, an attractive man, care about me."

"There's nothing wrong with that. I'm just suggesting you hold off a bit. Don't get into something until you're sure it's what you really want. No need to rush into things."

"No, you're right, there isn't. You know, I do have to fly back to New York. Jack's business partners have put together a memorial service now that his body has been finally released for cremation. I'll have to go and play the grieving widow. Jack's lawyers wanted me to stay around some, to talk about all the financial stuff. I was hoping to put that part off—the thought of staying at our apartment there for too long just, just . . . well, even with Mrs. Hanson there with me, it would seem awful cold and depressing.

"It was startin' to feel a bit nicer here, especially with the party last night. Well, most of it. So I didn't want to stay in New York. But I suppose the better thing to do right now, the grown-up thing to do, would be to get things settled, and maybe take time to get my head together, like you said."

Leslie looked at Maggie, as if for approval, and Maggie smiled.

"I think that's a good idea. You can always come back, you know."

"Yes, I can. And I could always close up that apartment in New York and move somewhere else too. Somewhere warm. I'm a southern girl, you know. I've never gotten used to these cold winters. Maybe I could even get back into modeling. But I don't need the money. I'd only take the jobs I really wanted."

It sounded to Maggie like Leslie was beginning to realize she could take charge of her own life, and not simply depend on someone to take care of her. That was good. Just a beginning, but still good.

Something Maggie's mother used to say popped into her head: Long journeys began with small steps. She glanced at Leslie's shoes—high heeled, open-toed mules, quite a bit on the flimsy side. Maggie hoped they were up to the trip.

Maggie left Leslie's house with a full stomach and a slightly easier mind, as well as a couple of plastic containers of party leftovers Leslie insisted she take. She doubted she had learned anything that would help her solve Jack and Alexander's murders. But she had at least firmly crossed off one name from her list of possible suspects. Leslie's name had been mostly erased anyway. But the clincher for Maggie had been when she asked Leslie straight out who she thought had poisoned her husband.

Leslie had looked at Maggie with steady eyes. "I don't know, Maggie. But I'm sure as can be it wasn't Elizabeth, and I told the sheriff so. That may be making him look at me a lot closer, but I don't care. As long as he stops worryin' that poor girl."

Maggie put her car in gear and pulled away from the Warwick home for the second night in a row. Tonight hers had been the only car parked in front, and traffic was nearly non-existent. As she made the U-turn to head back home her headlights swung over a dark figure standing across the street against some trees.

A late-night jogger pausing to catch his breath? Someone walking her dog? Except the sidewalks were pretty icy for jogging, and Maggie saw no leash or dog. She mulled this over, feeling uneasy until she pulled into the cabin's driveway. Once again the cabin's windows looked down on her ominously through the dark. Maggie shivered, and regretted for a moment having let Dyna go.

She pulled into the garage and climbed out of the car, locked the garage door, and hurried across the few feet to the cabin's steps. She was glad she had thought to leave a single lamp lit so that at least she wouldn't be stepping into a totally dark house.

Maggie slammed the cabin's door firmly and shot the deadbolt, feeling instantly better. As she turned around, though, movement at the edge of the stairs caught her eye, and she gasped for breath.

Ali meowed and marched up to her, seemingly as happy to see her as she was to realize it was him. When her heartbeat returned to normal, Maggie reached down and swept the large cat up in her arms, nuzzling her face into his fur.

"Feeling lonely, boy? So am I. How about we stick together the rest of the night?"

Ali purred.

Chapter Twenty

Maggie woke slowly the next morning, disturbing dreams lingering in her consciousness. Dreams that sprang from nightmarish memories. It was summer. She had been tied up and left alone in a dark, strange place, frantic to escape before a faceless killer returned.

Maggie tried to stir and found that, as on that summer night, she could not move. The realization jolted her fully awake, only to recognize that as well as being immobile she was not alone. Heavy breathing sounded in her ear.

Maggie's heart stopped. Then the fishy smell of cat food wafted to her. She lifted her head, wrinkling her nose. Ali lay beside her, having taken her up on last night's impulsive offer of togetherness, and made himself at home on the bed, weighing the covers down tightly next to her with his bulk. Since the other edge of the sheet was tucked firmly under the mattress, Maggie was effectively pinned down. At first relief flooded her as her heart resumed its regular beat. Then grumpy annoyance moved in as she struggled to get loose. Her flailings failed to dislodge the immovable cat, who had apparently staked a claim on that portion of her bed.

"Don't let me disturb you," Maggie muttered, when she managed to sit up enough to lean over to his ear. Ali nuzzled deeper into the comforter, oblivious to her sarcasm. Maggie gave up and climbed out of bed. She pulled the window curtain aside to let the light in and saw snow falling. Lots of it.

The sight wasn't as thrilling as it had been the other morning, when Dyna had cheerfully called her attention to the new snowfall. For one thing, Maggie was alone, except for Ali. And for another, the snow was still coming down, heavily, which was disconcerting since she had no idea how long that would continue and what that would mean to her for the day ahead.

Well, nothing could be done about it, so she shuffled into her robe and slippers, ran her fingers through her tousled hair, and prepared to face the day.

Downstairs, not feeling hungry after last night's feast with Leslie, Maggie simply set up a pot of coffee to perk, then dutifully filled Ali's food and water bowls. As the coffeemaker gurgled and hissed, she wandered over to the sliding glass door, hands in pockets, and looked out at the snow. A bleak feeling of isolation crept over her.

Although she knew she was walking distance—granted, not easy walking distance, especially now—from the town's main street, here on Hadley Road she was the only resident. And now, with Dyna away and only a sleeping cat for company, and with heavy snow cutting her off at least temporarily from other people, Maggie felt her aloneness keenly. She rubbed her arms, feeling cold, although she knew the cabin's temperature hadn't changed.

Suddenly she shook her head. *Enough!* she told herself. You told Dyna you were used to being on your own, and you are. This is not a big problem. Maggie turned back to the kitchen with determined energy. If she couldn't go out, she would have plenty to keep her occupied. She'd work on her book. And when she couldn't write anymore, she'd clean the house. Wash windows. Anything. And before she knew it Dyna would call to tell her all she had been doing in Atlantic City.

The coffeemaker hissed its final hiss, and she poured out a mugful of coffee and blew on it, eager to take her first sip. She was anxious to get started and chase away the doldrums.

Ali looked up through slitted, disapproving eyes as Maggie switched on the vacuum cleaner in her bedroom. He remained prone on the bed, and tolerated the disturbance warily as long as it kept beyond two feet of his nesting quarters. But when Maggie began bumping the edge of the bed with the noisy cleaner, Ali jumped up, not troubling to hide his contempt for her lack of consideration, and stalked out of the room.

A load of wash was chugging in the washer and one spinning in the dryer as Maggie vacuumed the entire upstairs area. The carpets hadn't been in dire need of cleaning, except for the likely deposits of cat hair in the last twenty-four hours, but Maggie needed noise, as well as the activity of vacuuming.

She had worked on her book for most of the morning, until the silence began to get to her. She swore she could hear the individual flakes landing outside as the snow continued to come down. The phone had been disturbingly silent as well, even when Maggie stared right at it.

What was Dyna doing? she wondered. Was she okay? When was she going to call? Along with that thought had come uneasy ones about Rob. They hadn't actually talked for a long time now—Maggie had lost track. They each seemed to call only when the other was out. Should she try again? What if she just got his answering machine? A stubbornness crept up that kept her from doing anything other than postponing the decision. And so she tried to keep busy.

When work at the computer didn't occupy her mind enough, when she had run out of ideas and simply sat staring at the screen, she turned it off and sought out the cleaning supplies again.

Maggie scrubbed floors and polished tabletops until her nervous energy finally ran out. Then she collapsed on the living room sofa. Ali, who had been lurking in a dark corner, immediately scooted over and made an attempt to climb up with her, but Maggie pushed him firmly away.

"We've had enough togetherness for a while. You belong to Dyna, you know. You'll just have to wait for her to come back."

After trying one more time and being deterred, the large cat gave up and wandered over to his food bowl. He gobbled a bite or two, then played with the crunchy bits, scooping pieces out of his bowl with a curved paw and scooting them around Maggie's clean floor, hockey style. Maggie swore he looked over his shoulder to catch her reaction.

She sighed, too tired to get up and stop him. "You're a devious little thing, just like Leslie said. Go ahead, have your revenge. But just wait until you're hungry again, and see how you like searching for your food all over the cabin."

The tip of Ali's tail flicked, and he moved over to his water bowl, testing it with a paw as if deciding what he could do with it. Maggie closed her eyes, not wanting to know. She reached for the afghan that had been draped over the back of the sofa, pulled it around her, and breathed deeply.

The next thing she knew, the phone was ringing and it had grown dark out.

"Maggie? Hello? Is that you?"

"Mmmph." Maggie coughed, snuffled, then said, "Dyna?"

"Did I wake you?"

Maggie straightened up, letting the afghan fall away. The only light in the room came from the overhead in the kitchen, but she clearly saw Ali's face gazing at her from the foot of the couch, the front half of his body on the edge of the afghan. It might have been a trick of the light, but the look on his face seemed definitely smug.

"Little devil," she muttered.

"What? What did you say, Maggie?"

"Nothing. How's it going, Dyna?"

"Great. Pam and I have been busy. She left the baby with her mother-in-law, and we've been tramping all over Atlantic City. Like I said, a lot of her neighbors work there, so we talked to several of them."

"What did you find out?"

"Well," Dyna took a deep breath, and Maggie, hearing the flutter of paper, pictured her reading from a notebook of scribblings. "First of all, Alexander—no surprise here—was well known as a big gambler. He ran up some pretty big debts, and he almost always stayed at Jack Warwick's hotel."

"That's interesting."

"It's called the Turtlewick. Jack owned it in partnership

with someone named Turtletaub. The original name of the hotel was going to be something like 'The Green Turtle,' but Jack, of course, had to get his name in there somehow. Anyway, people at the hotel knew Alexander. He ate in the restaurant there a lot—someone said he was a big tipper. But there didn't seem to be any sign of an affair going on. They said he was hardly ever seen with the same people twice, and a lot of the time he was alone. That probably blows my theory of a Mafia princess mistress."

"I guess so. Did anyone see Alexander with Jack?"

"I asked about that. They did remember seeing them once or twice, having dinner together. Just before Jack and Leslie came up to Cedar Hill."

"I wonder if Alexander made the first move to Jack about buying Big Bear."

"Could be. Maybe Alexander made big promises about being able to get the zoning changed and arrange the sale."

"Mmm." Maggie wondered what that might have to do with the eventual murders of both men.

"Everyone we talked to, by the way, knew about Jack's playing around, his 'womanizing,' as someone put it. Said he was pretty open about it, even hitting on hotel employees. His partner was getting pretty ticked off, they said. He felt they lost some good workers, people in upper management and all, because of it."

"I'm sure they did." Poor Elizabeth. If she had only known. "What about Leslie? Where was she? Was she ever seen with Alexander?"

"You mean just the two of them? No, there was nothing like that. And I don't think she was with them when Jack and Alexander were seen talking. That sounded like a private kind of business thing. Leslie only seemed to be around when there were these big to-do's for the hotel, you know, entertaining the bigwigs to drum up business for the hotel. Being the hostess."

"Hmm."

"Tomorrow we're going to talk to people at the casinos. Maybe we can dig up something there."

"Okay. You're doing a great job. Just be careful."

"No problem. What's happening up there? I heard on the weather news you got some more snow."

"Yeah, enough to keep me inside today. I'm not crazy about driving in deep snow with my Cavalier. But," Maggie craned her head to look out the window, "I think it's stopped, so the roads should be okay soon. I'll go into town tomorrow, see what I can dig up."

"Great. How's Ali doing?"

Maggie looked over at Ali, who had inched even further onto the afghan while she had been talking. She thought about the scare he had given her that morning, and the cat food scattered into the far corners of the cabin. And who knows what other surprises he had arranged while she slept.

"Ali's terrific," she said, her voice taking on the forced enthusiasm she used when trying to talk positively to parents of particularly difficult students. "Just super."

"Oh, good. Give him a big hug for me," Dyna instructed, and signed off.

Maggie looked at the orange cat. He gazed calmly back at her.

"It seems I owe you a hug."

Ali blinked contentedly.

Chapter Twenty-one

The next morning Maggie looked out at bright sun shining on clean, white snow. The plow had cleared Hadley Road and much of the cabin's driveway. All Maggie had to do was clear the pile of snow pushed up close to the garage door and she could be on her way into town.

Last night she had decided to talk to Annette, who didn't seem to miss a thing as far as the town's business was concerned. Surely she would have information that would be helpful to Maggie, and to Elizabeth. And to the town, which, whether the townspeople realized it or not, was in serious trouble. Someone was living in their midst who had no qualms about killing.

The first murder, Jack's, may have been a long time in the planning. But the second, Alexander's, seemed impulsive, a hasty action possibly spurred by a greater urgency. It looked to Maggie as though the murderer was getting bolder and less cautious. What would he or she do next, to be rid of a perceived threat? How desperate was this person becoming?

She loaded her breakfast dishes in the dishwasher and rinsed out the coffee carafe. Ali's bowls had been attended to, but the cat still slept upstairs, this time in Dyna's bed. Maggie wondered if he were sulking, as she had kept her bedroom door closed against him last night. Dyna would be back before long, and he would get more than his share of pampering. He'd just have to wait.

She pulled on her boots and jacket, and grabbed her keys from the kitchen counter.

"So long, Ali," she called out, immediately feeling ridiculous for doing so, then tramped down the cabin steps and started shoveling.

Maggie backed her Cavalier out of the garage and drove cautiously down the scraped and sanded road towards town. Hers were the only tracks on the thin layer of snow that had blown onto the road after the snowplow had done its work. She drove past empty cabins with shuttered windows, and was glad to turn onto Main Street to see signs of life and activity. One full day of solitude had been enough for her.

She had looked up Annette's address, remembering Dyna's scramble for it a few days back. Timber Drive was easy to find, not far off Main, and when Maggie pulled up to number 238, she saw someone she thought might be Annette shoveling the front walk. She wasn't sure since the person stood knee-deep in snow, and wore a knitted, face-covering ski mask, topped with a pompom-festooned hat. The apple-red jacket, however, as well as the shape, was identifiable as Annette's, and Maggie climbed out of her car and called a greeting.

The masked figure looked up and set down the snow shovel.

"Well, hellooo." Annette's voice came through the mouth hole of the mask, and she stepped out of the snow onto a cleared portion of her walk. "And how are you?"

"I hate to interrupt you, but I wondered if I could talk to you a minute? About the murders?"

Annette whisked off her cap and ski mask at Maggie's last words, and beckoned Maggie toward the house. She was already bustling up her porch steps as she said, "Come in, come in. I'll fix us some nice tea."

By the time Maggie stepped through her front door, Annette had peeled off her snowy outerwear and was making clattering noises in the kitchen. "Just drop your things anywhere. Jason! Turn off those cartoons and go play in your room with your brother!"

A small boy about five years old darted out of the nearby family room and brushed by Maggie in his scramble to get up the stairs. Maggie heard a door slam above her as she pulled off her boots and jacket. She followed the clattering sounds to the kitchen and saw Annette pulling out cups and saucers, small plates, and utensils. A teakettle sat on one of her stove's burners, and a pound cake had been retrieved from its Tupperware dome.

"Please don't go to any trouble for me," Maggie protested.

Annette waved a hand impatiently. "No trouble at all. We'll be all set in two shakes of a lamb's tail. Sit down."

Maggie obeyed, pulling out a yellow-and-white vinyl-cushioned chair from the table. She looked around at the spotless kitchen as Annette scurried about, feeling somewhat bombarded with cheeriness from the daisy-printed wallpaper, duck-trimmed curtains, and framed embroidered mottos on the wall. The cake Annette plopped in front of her, however, looked good.

The teakettle whistled, and Annette filled the teapot, centering it on the table as she settled herself across from Maggie.

"Now, what was it you wanted to know?"

"What's been happening in connection with Alexander's death?" Maggie asked.

Annette's face took on such a businesslike expression Maggie eerily felt as though she were facing a school superintendent preparing to expound on the next year's budget. "The sheriff's been busy," Annette began. "He and his men, as you probably know, visited every house in town right after Alexander was discovered."

Maggie nodded.

"They said they were checking on everyone's well-being, but I think they were also checking for alibis."

Maggie remembered Elizabeth telling her the deputy had asked if she had been out early that day. He probably had looked for fresh footprints in the snow, as well as other signs.

"Did they come up with anything?"

Annette took a breath, said, "Indeed they did," then looked into the teapot. She pulled out a dripping tea ball, then poured out a cup of golden brown tea for each of them. Maggie waited, aware of how Annette enjoyed building up the suspense. Finally, she continued.

"Paul Dekens, it seems, had been out early that morning."

"Paul!"

"Yes, Paul. He *said*, from what I've heard, that he went to Big Bear to work on some papers."

"But nobody was there who can confirm it?"

"No one." Annette smiled. "Sugar?"

Maggie shook her head. This would be terrible news to Elizabeth. Elizabeth had feared Paul would be a suspect. He had strong motives for both murders, and now apparently opportunity as well.

"Paul has been to the sheriff's office, accompanied by his lawyer, I'm told." Annette shook her head as though in dismay, her lips pressed grimly, but the light in her eyes reflected an inner excitement. "Such a terrible thing. Now, I'm not saying Alexander deserved to be shot, but, you know, he did bring a lot of this on himself. The life he was leading! If he hadn't been murdered, he would have killed himself eventually."

"Do you mean suicide?"

"Oh, no. He'd never have done anything as thoughtful as that. I mean his drinking would have killed him. His drinking and driving. Why, I saw him myself, walking past here at three in the morning one night. It was the night that poor Mrs. Morgan was killed, driving on icy roads. I was up because of my youngest, Jason, being sick with the croup. I could hardly believe it when I happened to look out and there he was, Alexander Dekens, tramping up the hill. More cake?"

Maggie shook her head.

Annette cut a slice for herself then continued. "I thought I was seeing things at first, but it was him. Drunk as could be, weaving and grabbing on to things. I watched him all the way up to Piney Grove, where he turned toward his house and I couldn't see him anymore. Turned out he had plowed his car into a snow bank at the bottom of Main. Just left it there and walked on home. Why, he could have fallen down somewhere and frozen to death. No one would have found him until the next day."

Annette took a sip of tea. "You know, I never even got a chance to tell anyone about that, because first thing the next morning we all heard about Brenda Morgan's accident. Terrible thing."

Maggie thought Annette looked somewhat miffed that a juicy piece of gossip had been trumped by an even bigger story.

A series of loud thumps sounded on the ceiling. "Jason, Jeffrey! Don't make me come up there!" The thumping ceased, and Annette forked a piece of cake daintily. "By the way, how is Dyna enjoying Atlantic City?"

Maggie's surprise must have shown because Annette smiled sweetly with a hint of triumph. "Someone I know just happened to see her at the airport in Boston."

Good Lord, Maggie thought, she's got a network of spies checking in with her. "Actually," Maggie said, "she's visiting a friend who lives in New Jersey."

"That's nice. Most people I know go to New Jersey this time of year for the casinos—"

"Annette," Maggie interrupted to avoid a discussion of what Dyna might or might not be doing, "I've been thinking back to the night of the town meeting. I'm sure the sheriff asked if you saw anything strange happen just before Jack got sick."

"Oh, yes he certainly did, and no, I'm afraid I didn't." Annette's voice was filled with regret that she had missed this once-in-a-lifetime opportunity.

"I wondered, was anyone from town at the meeting who wouldn't normally have been?"

Annette thought for a moment, chewing. "Well, it was a bigger turnout than we usually have. But then this was a special topic, and the whole town seemed to be interested."

"How did you feel about the zoning change, by the way? Did you want the sale of Big Bear to go through or not?"

Annette looked at Maggie with wide-open eyes. She seemed honestly surprised by the question. "Why, what would the sale of Big Bear have to do with me?" She began waving her hands in the air, tossing out the various points of the controversy. "Selling, buying, ski resorts, mining, the environment." She shook her head. "Those are others' concerns." She took a sip of her tea and looked at Maggie somewhat reproachfully.

"I try to keep out of other people's business."

Maggie had to park her car two blocks from the market. It seemed that a lot of people had run out of things at the same time, and the small lot and the street parking in front were full. As she walked down the hill, she thought about Paul having been out early the morning of Alexander's murder.

Could Paul be the murderer? It was a distressing thought, but Maggie couldn't ignore the strong possibility. Both murders had benefitted Paul by halting the sale of Big Bear. With Alexander dead, his stock would go to Karin, who certainly would side with Paul. And Maggie had seen plenty of tension and anger rather than brotherly love between the two.

But could Paul have planted the false evidence at Elizabeth's? Had the concern Maggie thought she had seen in Paul for Elizabeth all been a sham?

Maggie was so absorbed she almost didn't notice Vickie coming towards her, a bulky brown grocery bag clutched in her arms. As Vickie came nearer Maggie called out, "Since you're not working this must be Monday."

Vickie peered around the bag and grinned. "Yes, and see what fun I have in my leisure time."

"Ah, yes. Shopping for groceries has always been my idea of a good time too."

"Actually, I'll be stopping in at the restaurant to drop off a can of paprika. Dan's supply ran short yesterday, and he'll be starting some soup bases early tomorrow. I told him I wouldn't mind picking it up."

"That reminds me," Maggie said before Vickie could move on, "you said Dan ran a restaurant in Atlantic City. Did he ever mention seeing Alexander in it? I understand Alexander spent a lot of time at the casinos there."

Vickie shook her head. "Dan's not much of a chatterbox on the job, but I could ask him. I suppose Alexander could have come into his and Brenda's last place, the Terrapin. Alexander certainly came with Karin to the restaurant here a lot, but toward the end we all wished they didn't, or at least that he didn't. You were there that last time, weren't you? You and Dyna?"

Maggie nodded. She remembered well the tension in the room, as Alexander drunkenly hinted at a relationship between Dan and Karin. With a husband like that, few would have blamed Karin if she actually had looked for comfort elsewhere. However, Maggie didn't believe that had been the case.

Vickie had started walking again, then stopped to say, "I hear Mrs. Warwick will be leaving us—going back to New York for the memorial service, but not coming back like she planned." Probably because Maggie looked surprised, Vickie explained, "She called Dan to tell him at the restaurant yesterday. Things were slow, because of the snow, and I was nearby when he got the call. I could tell he wasn't happy to hear it. I'm kinda disappointed myself. I thought they just might be good for each other."

"You think so?"

"Yeah, well, she's so lively and he's so quiet, and he seemed to be helping her in a way."

Maggie remembered Dan steering Leslie away from the bar at the party, and nodded. "Maybe she'll come back to Cedar Hill," she said.

"Yeah, maybe. Well, see you!"

Maggie walked on to the market and joined the throng shopping for food. She needed only a few things—milk, bread, fruit-flavored sourballs. Her supply of essentials had run low. She wound her way through the aisles, found what she wanted, and got into the express check-out line.

It was when she was leaving the store that she encountered Regina, who did not look happy.

"Good morning," Maggie said, smiling tentatively.

"Hmmph! Not much good happening lately, is there?" Maggie was wondering what to reply to that when Regina said, "Go see Elizabeth."

"Elizabeth?"

"I just came from there. She doesn't look good."

"Okay. Sure." Maggie was just starting to think pleasant

thoughts about Regina's thoughtfulness when she suddenly found herself on the receiving end of a piercing glare.

"We don't need more busybodies here!"

"Excuse me?"

Regina glared a few more seconds to make her point, then stomped around Maggie and pushed her way into the grocery store, leaving Maggie dumbfounded.

"What in the . . . ?"

Maggie stared after her, open-mouthed, and briefly considered following Regina into the store. She quickly rejected the thought, remembering the crowd of potential eavesdroppers inside. Instead, she turned and continued on to her car. When she came close enough to pull out her keys, she saw Annette and Vickie, standing near the corner chatting. The last two people Maggie had been talking to. The last two she had been asking questions of concerning Alexander.

Regina must have passed by them. Had she heard what they were discussing? What had they been discussing?

And what would that mean for Maggie?

Chapter Twenty-two

Maggie pulled up to the Book Nook, still frowning over Regina's comment. She climbed out of the car and clambered over the snow piled high at the curb, thinking that the problems in the town seemed to be growing as fast as these mounds of snow. As she tramped around to Elizabeth's back door she wished she could clear those problems as easily as the snowplow had cleared her driveway. Or that they would simply melt away, along with the snow, with the arrival of spring. Unfortunately, it wouldn't be that simple. She tapped on her friend's door.

"Maggie, I'm so glad you came," Elizabeth said, tension evident in her wrinkled forehead, her eyes looking troubled. She stepped back to let Maggie in, and as Maggie shucked her jacket asked, "Did you hear about Paul?"

"Yes," Maggie said, turning from the coat rack, "but I wouldn't worry just yet. Not having an alibi doesn't automatically lead to a charge."

"I hate knowing he's going through this, though. It's bad enough, his own brother being killed"—Maggie noticed how Elizabeth avoided the word *murdered*—"but to have questions, insinuations on top of that. It's just too awful."

"It doesn't seem that long ago that Paul was worried for the same reasons about you."

Elizabeth clenched her hands together. "The whole situation is terrible. This used to be such a wonderful community. Now people are dying and we're all peering at each other with suspicion. When is it all going to end?" She sat down and rubbed at her face.

"Soon, I'm sure," Maggie said, wishing very much she had something more concrete to offer. She looked toward the kitchen and, remembering the comfort effect of Dyna's pancakes, asked, "When's the last time you ate? Can I fix some tea?"

Elizabeth looked up over her fingers and managed a smile. "Let me get it. And don't worry, I have plenty of food. Regina dropped off another casserole, though I've begged her to stop doing that." She glanced at the clock. "It's just about lunch time. Want to join me?"

"Sure. I was just planning to have a sandwich at home. If Regina's casserole looks as good as the one I saw her fixing the other day, I'd love to try it."

Maggie made tea while Elizabeth doled out two platefuls of Regina's veggie and cheese concoction and warmed them in the microwave. They took their plates to the couch to hold on their laps, setting their mugs on the end tables.

As they ate Maggie chatted about anything unconnected to the murders, eventually getting around to Dyna's recent acquisition of Ali and some of his mischief. The tension in Elizabeth's face gradually eased. She laughed over Ali, and brought up old memories of a dog she had owned as a child. The time, as well as their lunch, disappeared quickly.

"Regina knows how to put a good dish together," Maggie said, scraping up her final forkful. "She might not be too pleased to know I had some of it, though. I seem to have made her angry today."

"I find it hard to tell when she's not angry. But what did you do?"

"Well," Maggie began, as Elizabeth took her plate from her, "I needed to know what's been going on since Alexander was shot, and went to ask Annette. I'm afraid she may have been talking about our conversation sooner than I expected, and that Regina may have overheard her. I should have gone right to John, I suppose. He wouldn't have mentioned it to anyone else. But then, neither would he have told me anything."

"I'm sorry for John," Elizabeth said. "I know he has his job to do, but he cares about the people here. All this probably hurts him as much as anyone."

"By the way," Maggie said, "John and Dyna seem to have something starting between them."

Elizabeth smiled at that, looking interested.

"Unfortunately, though, as far as that's concerned anyway, she's off in Atlantic City right now. She's checking into what Alexander's activities were when he was there. With a bit of luck, she might dig up something helpful." Maggie suddenly had an idea. "Elizabeth, why don't you come stay with me while she's gone?"

Elizabeth looked over at her and shook her head. "No, I think I'd be very poor company for anyone right now."

"You don't have to be great company. I have Ali for that," Maggie said, smiling. "But why should we both be alone? Come on over."

Elizabeth smiled. "I can't. Not now. I just have to be by myself. Don't worry, I'll be fine."

Maggie sighed, and, looking at Elizabeth's determined face, gave up. She knew Elizabeth wasn't "fine," but simply hanging on, day by day. Visits and distractions might relieve her pressures for a while, but they were only temporary. She required a much more permanent fix. Elizabeth needed her life back, and soon. Maggie had to get busy.

With that thought in mind, Maggie stood up and began gathering her things. "The milk I left out in the car is probably close to freezing by now, so I'd better go before the cap pops. Promise to at least think about coming over?"

"I will."

They hugged, and Maggie left after extracting a second promise that Elizabeth would call if she needed her.

Out in her car, Maggie sat quietly and thought. Making up her mind, she put the car in gear and pulled away from the curb. She didn't know what good it would do, but she was at least going to try. She headed for the sheriff's office.

* * *

John didn't look particularly happy to see her when Maggie walked in, but he greeted her politely. His deputy had ushered Maggie into John's office without questioning her on her need to see him, and Maggie wondered if that would get him a chewing out later. John looked harried, and Maggie realized she'd better be quick and to the point.

"I hear you're looking at Paul now in the murder investigation," she said.

John rubbed his face and folded his hands on the desk. "I'm not even going to ask where you heard that," he said.

Maggie shrugged. "It's a small town, John. People talk, rumors fly. I just want to know if this means you're not looking at Elizabeth anymore."

"There were two murders, you know. So far we have a suspect for each."

"But . . ." Maggie swallowed what she was going to say, knowing it would do little good. "Will you at least tell me this? I can probably get it from Elizabeth's lawyer anyway, but you can save me the trouble. What was in the bottle you found in Elizabeth's cupboard. Was it poison?"

John nodded, his face stone-like. "Oleander. An extract from the plant. The same thing that killed Jack Warwick."

It was Maggie's turn to nod now. No real surprise there. The question that still remained, as far as she was concerned, was exactly how that bottle ended up at Elizabeth's.

John's phone buzzed, and he answered it quickly and hung up. "Did Dyna come with you?" he asked, getting to his feet.

"Dyna's gone to visit a friend in New Jersey for a couple days," Maggie said, remaining seated. "She stopped in at Atlantic City and happened to run into a few people who knew Alexander."

John sighed heavily. "Why don't you join her there? I hear it's an interesting place." He was moving toward the door, signaling that the visit was ended.

"I find Cedar Hill pretty interesting. Sometimes I hear very curious things." John looked close to the end of his patience, so Maggie stood up slowly saying, "For instance, I heard a tale of the night Alexander drove into a snow bank and staggered the rest of the way home drunk. It was the night of Brenda Morgan's accident."

"Yes, I remember that. Her blood alcohol tested pretty high, and we briefly considered that she had been out drinking with Alexander. But we were able to track his movements that night and could place him far from town, and not with her, that entire night."

"Where had he been?" Maggie asked.

At that moment the door opened, and John's deputy leaned his head in, murmuring something inaudible to Maggie. John turned to her and said, "You can ask Karin for that information, if you like. But I don't think she'd appreciate the reminder, at this time, of her husband's foolishness. Now if you'll excuse me . . ." John held the door open for Maggie, who had no choice but to exit through it.

She thanked him politely for his time and left, pondering some of the things he had said. He seemed to be treating the two murders as unconnected, which disturbed Maggie. She was convinced they had been committed by the same person. But how was she going to prove it?

She climbed into her car and shook her milk to see if it was still liquid. There was a definitely slushy sound to it. It was time to get it home.

With her mind running over the many things she had heard that day, Maggie pulled into the cabin's garage. She carried her groceries into the cabin, kicked off her boots in the foyer, and unpacked the bag. As she moved about the small kitchen automatically, her thoughts only partially on what she was doing, she suddenly felt a cold wetness seeping through her socks from the kitchen floor and looked down in surprise. Melted snow had puddled there.

But she hadn't walked into the kitchen with her boots on, had she? Had snow dripped off her jeans? Or from her jacket? She didn't know. Maggie felt an uneasiness she couldn't explain, and shrugged it off, grabbing a paper towel to mop up the water. She warned herself to keep her mind on one thing at a time, before she started walking into doors.

Or worse.

Chapter Twenty-three

Maggie turned over in bed. She pulled the comforter close to her head, feeling cold. In a moment she pushed it off, feeling too hot. The room was pitch dark. She wondered what time it was, but the effort of lifting her head a few inches to see her travel clock on the end table seemed enormous. She felt awful.

She remembered feeling odd sometime around midnight. No, even earlier than that. She'd felt a queasiness as she had worked at her laptop. But it came and went, and she presumed it would eventually go away altogether. Instead, it had gradually worsened. Maggie threw back the covers and made a mad dash for the bathroom, heaving.

She returned to the bedroom on rubbery legs. She felt the room spin and collapsed onto the bed. Her head pounded. Was it the flu? She had had the flu before and this was worse. Much worse.

Her face itched. She raised one limp hand and scratched at it. Then her waist itched. Her leg. Her back. Soon Maggie was scratching uncontrollably. Until it began to hurt. She felt a wetness on her fingers and crawled over to switch on the bedside lamp. Her fingertips were red. She had scratched until she drew blood.

What was happening!

Maggie thought back to all she had eaten lately. Dinner was a pasta dish she had brought back from Leslie's. She had sampled the same dish the night before when she and Leslie had raided the party leftovers. Surely it couldn't have gone bad in the short time it sat in the cabin's refrigerator, could it?

Lunch had been Regina's casserole that she had shared with Elizabeth. Was Elizabeth sick? Should she call her?

She pulled herself to a sitting position. Dizziness rocked her and she put her head on her knees until it passed. The phone on the end table was an old Princess model. She grabbed at the receiver, putting it to her ear. No dial tone. The whirling in Maggie's head heightened her confusion and she struggled to clear it enough to think. Could Ali have pulled the jack out of the wall? She leaned to the back of the end table, pulling it out a few inches. The jack was firmly in place. But the phone was dead. Her stomach churning, Maggie thought of the phone downstairs. Would it work? She'd have to find out.

After waiting for a wave of nausea and wooziness to pass, she stood, shakily, then staggered to the door. Maggie leaned against the door frame, breathing hard. Nearly every part of her was urging her to go back to the bed, collapse onto it, give up. But her brain told her no. It would be so easy, but she must resist. Something was wrong, terribly wrong, and she couldn't give in to it. She had to move.

Maggie eased the door open, bracing her weight on it and stepped into the hall. She flicked on the hall light, then grabbed onto the wrought-iron railing for support, following it to the staircase. Sinking to a sitting position, she eased herself down, step by step, the only way to keep from losing her balance and tumbling headfirst. Halfway down she had to stop as her head swam and eyes blurred. When it passed she continued on down.

Maggie made her way to the end table that held a lamp and the telephone. She nearly tipped the lamp over as she bumped into its shade, then fumbled for the switch and turned it on. Leaning heavily on the table, she reached for the phone and put the receiver to her ear. No dial tone.

Maggie sank onto the sofa. What was going on?

The itching she had managed to ignore as she struggled

down the steps flared up again. She rubbed at her skin, trying desperately to avoid scratching with her nails, and groaned. Tears sprang to her eyes. She felt so bad, so very, very bad. And she needed help. How could she get it?

Dyna had a cellphone, but Maggie knew it had gone with her to Atlantic City. Why hadn't *she* gotten herself one? She'd meant to, many times. It had crossed her mind as she prepared to drive up here from Baltimore. But she hadn't gotten around to it. And now she needed it. Badly. What was she going to do?

The itching receded, only to be replaced by a severe pain in her head. Maggie leaned back against the cushion. She closed her eyes and saw flashes of light behind her eyelids. This was not the flu, she realized. And she didn't think it was spoiled food. The itching seemed to point to an allergic re-action, but not along with the other symptoms she was having.

Maggie thought, trying hard to focus over the pounding in her head. Her heart beat rapidly, and her chest rose and fell as her lungs gasped for air, trying to keep up with it. This wasn't an ordinary illness. She knew that. Her body was tell-ing her that. But could she believe what else it was trying to tell her? Was it possible? Had she been poisoned?

The thought overwhelmed her. Maggie sat, immobile, her mind racing to find other explanations, something it could cope with. She remembered the puddle on the kitchen floor she had stepped into that afternoon. It hadn't been from her own boots. Had someone been in the cabin while she was out, poisoning the food in her refrigerator? Her hands began to shake and beads of sweat broke out on her forehead.

Nothing else made sense. She had to face it. But what had she been poisoned with? It wasn't the same thing that had been given to Jack Warwick. It wasn't oleander. If it had been, she knew she would be dead by now. But what was it and how fast acting was it? How much time did she have to live?

Maggie clenched her hands to stillness, then wiped away the sweat. She needed to think rationally, not panic. She began to assess the situation. First: she was still conscious. Dizziness constantly threatened her, but so far she had been able to fight it back. Second: her eyes still focused. Third: she was still fairly mobile.

She had no idea how much longer these assets would last. She needed to act now. While she could. Drag herself to her car, which was locked in the garage, and drive into town. Could she do it? She had to. It could make the difference between life or death.

She pulled herself off the sofa and staggered to the kitchen counter. Her keys, thankfully, sat at the end of it where she usually left them. There was no point trying to dress. What she had on, sweatpants and long-sleeved tee, would have to do. Somehow she managed to get her bare feet into her boots, and pull on her jacket. She rested on one of the high stools for a minute, gathering her strength, then went to the door and pulled it open.

Maggie took one step out onto the side landing when she heard a loud crack, and something zinged into the wooden railing, sending splinters flying. She pulled herself back inside quickly. Someone had shot at her!

The shock of that sent her staggering into the foyer wall. Someone was out there, with a rifle. Had been waiting for her to try to leave the cabin. Planned to keep her inside, to die by poison. Or to shoot her if she tried to leave!

No, it couldn't be. Maggie couldn't believe it. It had to be her muddled head tricking her. Or maybe not. She had to be sure.

Maggie stumbled to the kitchen and scrambled through the kitchen drawers. She found a long spoon and stuck it into her knit cap. Pulling the door open again, which spilled light onto the landing, she poked the hat out. Another crack sounded as a bullet zinged past, this time hitting nothing. Someone was out there, keeping her hostage, waiting for her to die.

Now she had two choices: death by poison or death by a bullet. Which one did she want? She sank onto a stool and leaned her head on the kitchen counter. Within seconds she popped it up. Neither! She wasn't going to give up. She was going to survive this. Maggie managed a grim laugh. Or die trying.

Her mind raced, searching for answers, coming up only with questions. First question: who was out there?

Just a few hours ago, Maggie had struggled with much the same problem: who was the murderer? She had listed names, listed motives and opportunities, and come up with nothing. Or nothing that had totally convinced her. Now, however, she had one more thing, one terrible thing, to add to her knowledge of this person. This killer had become so fearful of what she had been doing, how close she was getting, that he had become desperate enough to come after her in this manner. That clinched it for Maggie. Now she was sure she knew who it was.

But what was she going to do about it?

Ideas bounced around the pain in her head, too often losing their way in the muddle the poison was making of her brain. She grappled to hold onto them, trying desperately to think clearly. She had few options, she knew. Having no weapons to fight back with, she had only her wits left. She had to think. She had to get out of this alive.

Maggie dragged herself off the kitchen stool. Stumbling back to the door, she shot the deadbolt, then opened the small utility closet next to the foyer. She found the circuit breaker box Dyna had shown her that first day, and opened the metal cover, pulling the main breaker. The cabin immediately plunged into darkness.

She let her eyes adjust to the darkness for a moment, then, using the faint moonlight coming through the glass doors as well as her memory of the cabin's layout, found her way back to the circular stairway. A groan welled up from deep inside her as she grasped the railing. She felt as though she were at the foot of Mount Everest. But she had to do it. Step by step, inch by inch, Maggie pulled herself up the wrought-iron staircase, abdominal pains now stabbing along with the pain reeling through her head. Her body temperature alternated between feverish and chilled, never staying at one point long enough for her to decide to throw off her jacket or zip it up. When she finally neared the top, she sat, resting her head and shoulders on the last step, gathering her strength.

The urge to sleep wrapped around her like a warm blanket, but Maggie fought it, pulling herself up by the final step. She staggered into her room, aiming for the window that faced Hadley Road and the woods beyond.

She unlocked the sash and, grunting with effort, pulled it upwards. Freezing air rushed at her, shocking her flagging senses to the alertness she needed. She sank to the floor at one side of the open window, kneeling, and took a deep breath, calling out with all the strength she could muster.

"Dan Morgan! I know you're out there!"

Chapter Twenty-four

Silence greeted Maggie. The absolute silence of a winter night. Maggie waited, her eyes straining to see something, anything, through the dark from the edge of the window. She turned to see the battery-powered travel clock beside the bed, now the only thing in the cabin that was lit. 5:42.

Maggie thought back to when she had eaten the pasta dish. Dan must have chosen that as the most likely thing for her to eat. Or maybe he dosed everything, she didn't know. But she had worked at her laptop for several hours, not hungry after sharing Regina's casserole with Elizabeth. She remembered hoping the phone would ring with a call from Dyna. Had the line been cut by then, she wondered, since no call had come?

Keeping busy, Maggie hadn't thought of food until at least nine or ten o'clock, much later than normal for her. Had Dan expected her to be ill much sooner? How long had he been waiting out there in the cold woods, ready to force her back into the cabin?

Maggie knew now he had somehow got into the cabin yesterday, perhaps while she was at John's. Dan had left his tracks in the kitchen—the melted snow she had stepped in later and shrugged off. A major error. Talking to Annette, however, had been her first error. Unable to keep anything to herself, Annette must have passed on their conversation to Vickie, who was on her way to the restaurant to deliver paprika. Vickie had probably told Dan what she had just heard.

Why hadn't Maggie put the pieces together sooner? They had all been there, she realized now. Dyna had told her about Jack's "womanizing" among his own employees. His hotel was named the Turtlewick after its co-owners. Dan Morgan's restaurant in Atlantic City, Vickie told her, was the Terrapin.

Maggie would have kicked herself if she had the strength. Every Marylander knew the University of Maryland's mascot was the terrapin. A turtle. The Turtlewick Hotel would of course have a restaurant called the Terrapin. And Dan's wife helped him run it, and probably was one of Jack Warwick's conquests.

Dan waited a long time to get his revenge on Jack. Maggie thought he might not even have planned it until Jack suddenly showed up in Cedar Hill. By then Brenda Morgan was dead. By Vickie's account, she had been a non-drinker, but she was killed in a high blood alcohol-related car accident. Was it an accident, or had Dan arranged it by somehow getting her drunk and putting her behind the wheel?

Maggie knew she might never know, but had Alexander known? Had he seen something on that night after his own car plowed into a snow bank and he staggered drunkenly the rest of the way home? Had he actually seen something, or had Dan only feared he had seen, and remembered, something, and therefore had to be eliminated?

Unable to forgive his wife, who, coming with Dan to Cedar Hill obviously thought she had been forgiven, Dan must have kept his anger simmering until he found the perfect time to kill her—an icy night when the bad roads, plus her intoxication, would be blamed. He might even have gotten away with it until Jack Warwick appeared, stirring up Dan's fury once more. Jack likely had no idea who Dan was, since Dan's work kept him out of sight in the kitchen most of the time. But Dan knew who Jack was, and got his revenge.

Was making a play for Leslie part of Dan's revenge? Would that revenge have been all the sweeter if he could end up with Jack's wife and possibly his money? If so, Maggie had thrown a wrench into that plan, unknowingly. Was that another reason Dan wanted her dead?

Maggie took another deep breath and leaned to the edge of the window. "Dan, it won't work. I can wait."

Silence.

"I know you're out there, Dan. I can outlast you. Your plan isn't working."

More silence. Maggie leaned against the wall next to the window and grabbed short, quick breaths. She hoped she was managing to sound much stronger than she felt.

"You're nothing but a coward, Dan Morgan!" she called out. "You killed Jack and tried to pin it on Elizabeth. A coward! And stupid for thinking you can get away with it. Leslie is right to run from you." Maggie leaned back again, breathing heavily. She waited.

After what seemed like hours, he finally answered. "I could have had her. Except for you! She would have been mine. I could have cared for her."

Maggie called back quickly. "You would have cared for the money that came with her. Jack's money."

"No! I don't need his money. But he ruined my life. I deserved his life in return—everything that was his."

"His money, you mean. That's what it's all about. It's all greed with you, Dan. You're as bad as Jack was. You both wanted to grab everything you could. From everyone else."

"No!"

"You think you're better than him, that you had some right to destroy him. But you're two of a kind. Except you aren't as smart. You're just plain dumb. You've murdered twice, three times, and you're trying to kill me. But it won't happen and you won't get away with it. You'll end up in prison, on death row. With nothing."

A bullet flew through the open window, hitting the far wall. Maggie fell back, her heart pounding. But she couldn't stop now. She leaned back to the edge of the window.

"Killing your wife was part of the plan, wasn't it, Dan? She was simply an inconvenience, just in your way."

"She deserved to die!" Dan's voice had risen in pitch. "She lied," he cried. "She lied! She betrayed me."

"Of course she lied. Of course she betrayed you. Who wouldn't?"

"She pretended. Always pretending. Claiming innocence! I couldn't stand it! I had to kill her!"

"And Alexander knew, didn't he."

"He was always in the way."

"He saw you, didn't he? He knew you killed Brenda."

"She deserved to die!"

"Because she betrayed you? But why not? How could she ever have loved you? You're a fool, Dan. A coward and a fool! Who could love a fool?"

Silence again. Maggie listened, hardly breathing, every fibre of her body listening. Then she heard it. Footsteps running through the snow. Towards the cabin. He was coming. And fast.

Maggie had to move quickly now, fighting the weakness and her reeling head. She lurched painfully in the dark against the door frame, not daring to pause, moving frantically along the hallway wall to the wrought-iron stairway. She reached the first step when she heard it.

Thump!

He was at the side door, kicking at it.

Maggie's heart stopped, then beat again, double time. She dropped to the top step, sliding down the staircase as rapidly as she dared, head bouncing against the curving side railing, hands reaching blindly, backside thumping from step to step nearly as rapidly as Dan Morgan's foot kicked at the door. She had just reached the bottom of the staircase when a heart-stopping shot rang out. He had shot the lock off!

Maggie scrambled on all fours to the far end of the sofa. Crouching, she grabbed for the afghan draped on the top and flicked it over herself, hoping desperately that in the darkness she would blend into the shape of the sofa, invisible. It was all she could think to do in the small, open cabin. It was all she could do, and she prayed it was enough.

Dan burst through the door, then stopped at the edge of the kitchen, listening, possibly scanning the area. Maggie held her breath, pressing against the sofa as tightly as possible, all her senses alert as she fought to ignore the pain still attacking her from within. She felt a rush of icy air come down from the open window in her room and heard a crash. Had the wind blown something over? Or was it Ali? Maggie had forgotten all about him. Had he knocked against something in his own scramble for safety? She had barely formed the thought when she realized Dan had heard it too.

She heard his steps pound up the stairway and into her bedroom. Maggie immediately flung off the afghan. She might have only seconds to act. Could she do it?

Her own breath coming in spasms, Maggie heard Dan's grunts and bellows of fury above her as he failed to find her. She searched frantically through the shadows of the living room. Where was it? Where was it!

She heard a door slam against the wall above, then another crash and a piercing yowl. Ali.

Run, Ali! Run!

Maggie's fingers suddenly closed over what she wanted, and a rush of excitement coursed through her. She heard Dan's pounding steps as he charged from the bathroom to Dyna's room, to another closet, and finally back into the upstairs hall. She scrambled with shaking limbs to do what she had to do before he came down.

Maggie saw his dark shape loom at the top of the stairs as she stood in the shadows below, her hands reaching up to the side railing. Dan, holding his rifle in both hands, came running down the stairs, ready, she was sure, to find her there and kill her. But his legs encountered something unexpected. The fireplace poker Maggie had jammed between the wrought-iron decorative swirlings of each side railing caught him just above the ankles. He fell, full force, head slamming against the floor, rifle flying out of his hands.

Maggie leaped forward, grabbed the rifle and jumped back. Shaking now from fear as well as from whatever was eating away at her insides, she cocked the rifle and struggled to hold it steady as she aimed it at Dan. Light in the room had increased from faint moonlight to the dark grey of pre-dawn.

She could see Dan's shape on the floor, breathing but motionless. Then he began to stir.

"Stay right there, Dan," she ordered, her voice sounding strangled to her ears.

Dan groaned, his hands going to his head. His head lifted, and she saw it turn toward her, looking at her. Was he sizing up the situation? Calculating his chances? He pushed himself, grunting, to a sitting position.

"I have your gun, Dan. Believe me, I'll use it if you make me." But could she? Her hands were shaking, despite all her efforts to control them. Dan must see that. She saw him shift slightly, and she tensed. Would she be able to shoot if she had to? Would her fingers work? Most of all, could she take a life? She had to, to save her own. But could she?

Dan suddenly sprang up with an animal-like roar, lunging at her.

A shot rang out.

Maggie watched in horror, as he sank to the floor. He groaned, spasmed, then lay unmoving and lifeless. She looked at the rifle in her hands, then up to the broken side door that Dan had rushed through seemingly only seconds ago. Regina White stood there, framed in the grey light behind her, her gun pointed downward as she watched Dan Morgan's body for any signs of life. After a moment, satisfied, she returned Maggie's stunned gaze and spoke, softly, with a hint of sadness.

"Some people the world will be a whole lot better off without."

Chapter Twenty-five

Maggie awoke with a groan, gradually realizing she was in a hospital bed. She vaguely remembered figures in scrub suits working on her, pumping her stomach. Looking to her left, she saw the IV attached to her arm, dripping in precious fluid. She felt wrung out, but the awful pain, nausea, and dizziness were gone.

Had it all been a dream? A nightmare? She moved slightly on the bed and was instantly aware of acute soreness at scattered points of her body, shoulders, legs, but mainly backside. She pictured ugly bruises in those areas and knew exactly how they had come—not from any dream but from bouncing off walls and sliding for her life down that iron staircase.

Maggie tried to pull herself upward, but stopped when her rubbery arms buckled. She knew there must be an electric control for the bed somewhere, but decided the effort of looking for it outweighed the benefits for the moment. She tried to think back to how she had gotten here, but her memory seemed to have large holes in it.

She remembered Regina taking the rifle from her and ordering her onto the sofa. A few brusque questions, and then she was gone. The next thing Maggie remembered was being in the hospital emergency room, in the hands of those medieval torturers/life-saving saints.

Maggie had many unanswered questions left, and could only hope, immobile as she was at the moment, that someone would show up soon with a few answers. She closed her eyes at this thought and it seemed to her the next instant she was hearing Dyna's voice.

"Maggie! Maggie, are you okay?"

Maggie suppressed the groan begging to be released from her throat as awareness of her scattered pains returned with consciousness. She peeked at Dyna's worried face through squinted eyes.

"The doctors said you'd be all right, but how do you feel?"

Maggie opened her mouth to speak, managed only a croaking sound, then tried again. "Peachy keen."

Dyna's face lit up. "Really? I'm so glad. I felt so bad since I'm the one who got you into all this."

Maggie shook her head. "I got myself into it. Can you find the control that will raise up this bed?

Dyna fumbled around until she got Maggie elevated to a sitting position, then pulled a chair close to the bed rails and sat down herself. Maggie instantly felt better to have Dyna at her eye level. "When did you get back?" she asked.

"Just minutes ago. I drove like a maniac from the airport in Boston. When I couldn't get hold of you last night I figured it was a storm or something that knocked the lines down. But by this morning I was worried enough to call John. He told me what happened, pretty much. Why don't you have a cell phone, Maggie?"

"That's the first thing I'm buying when I get out of here."

"Thank heaven Regina goes out walking as early as she does."

Maggie remembered Dan's final lunge at her and, shuddering, wondered if she would be alive now, if not for Regina. "Does she always carry a gun with her?"

"She said she started to after Alexander was shot. She also said she was concerned about you, that your poking around might be 'stirring up the cesspool,' as she put it. She deliberately hiked toward the cabin just to look things over, like she's the town's unofficial security guard or something."

"I'm glad she feels that way," Maggie said, managing a weak smile.

"You look kinda beat," Dyna said. "Do you want to rest awhile?"

"Oh no, I'm . . . okay," Maggie said, having to take two breaths to get all the words out. She let her eyes close, just for a moment, and when she opened them again Dyna was gone, the sun was coming through her window at a different angle, and she realized she felt much better. The healing power of sleep.

Someone brought her a tray of broth, cranberry juice, and jello, and it actually tasted good. She was just polishing off the jello when Dyna knocked at the partially open door.

"Hi! You're looking better."

Maggie's hand went to her hair, and she wondered, for the first time, how she really did look.

"I dropped my things at Elizabeth's," Dyna said. "John still has the cabin roped off as a crime scene."

"How's Elizabeth doing?"

"She's okay. Of course she's more worried about you, and feels guilty about what you went through for her. The whole town is in a turmoil. I could hardly get away for people stopping me and wanting to know about you, and talk about Dan."

"What are they saying about Dan?"

"Well, now they're saying stuff like 'I had my suspicions about him,' but I don't think anyone really had a clue about him."

"He was a tortured man," Maggie said.

"Yeah. John told me what you told him about his killing his wife and all."

Maggie thought back, and the memory of talking to John at some point in the emergency room came back, dimly.

"The funny thing is, though," Dyna said, "it doesn't seem as though Brenda ever had an affair with Jack Warwick."

"What?"

"No. I got this from Vickie. She says Brenda told her Dan had become insanely jealous back in Atlantic City after learning she had been alone once or twice with 'someone.' She didn't name names to Vickie, but it must have been Jack. She insisted they were only discussing business connected with the restaurant. But Dan wouldn't believe her. She agreed to leave Atlantic City and come to Cedar Hill to mollify Dan, and she thought he had finally come around to believing her. And then he killed her after all."

Maggie grappled with this information. "So Dan killed his wife because of something he only imagined she had done?"

"Seems that way."

"And Jack, who was certainly not an innocent, ended up being murdered for the one thing he hadn't done?"

"Uh-huh."

Maggie thought back to the town meeting where Jack had been poisoned. She remembered the spirited debate that had gone on about the zoning change that would facilitate the sale of Big Bear. Dan Morgan had been pointed out as one of the owners of a business that would suffer if Cedar Hill changed from a ski town to a mining town. She remembered how he had sat there that night, grimly silent, not adding a word of protest against the change.

Maggie remembered Regina's comment later, at her house, that any clear-thinking person who cared about his life here would speak up against Jack Warwick's plan. That should have alerted Maggie to Dan Morgan. He never spoke up. He had kept silent during the debate, since he was going to put an end to Jack's plan that night.

She wished fervently that she had picked up on that clue inadvertently presented by Regina. Alexander might still be alive if she had, and everyone would have been spared much suffering.

"John's not mad at you anymore," Dyna said, interrupting Maggie's self-castigation.

"Oh?"

"Well, he is, kind of. But since you're still alive and the town murderer is done away with, he forgives you."

"Kind of him," Maggie said. But she understood John's difficulty. "Will he have some free time now to spend with you?"

"Pretty soon, I think." Dyna smiled. "Maybe I'll cook up a

nice vegetarian dinner for him. At his place. The cabin's probably going to take a while to get cleaned up."

"What time is it, by the way?" Maggie asked. "Did I just have lunch or dinner?"

"You had dinner. Which reminds me, I haven't had mine yet. I wanted to take Elizabeth out, to celebrate, but guess what? She's going over to Paul's. I've got my fingers crossed about those two. She wants to come see you too, later. Are you up to it?"

"I'm feeling better by the minute." Maggie suddenly straightened up. "Ali! Is he okay?"

"Oh, sure. He's at Elizabeth's right now."

Maggie sank back. "Get him something special from me, okay? He deserves some kitty caviar. He helped save my life last night."

"I sure will. Hey, I just thought of something. Do you suppose Dan was the one who poisoned Ali?"

Maggie thought that over. "He just might have. He probably knew how Leslie felt about Ali, and decided to get rid of him for her. I think by that time he was becoming obsessed with Leslie."

Dyna shook her head, looking distressed, and to turn her thoughts away from the painful path they were probably going down Maggie said, "Dyna, when you get Ali's caviar, would you mind picking up a hairbrush for me? And maybe . . ." Maggie ran down a short list of things, and Dyna, successfully distracted, made a note and promised to gather them all. She then took off to investigate the cuisine of the hospital cafeteria.

Left alone, Maggie mulled over what she had recently learned. So much misery, it seemed, had been brought about by relationships falling apart. What must have begun with much love and hope between two people had somehow disintegrated. Dan and Brenda, Karin and Alexander, Leslie and Jack. Had the foundations of each union been on such shaky ground from the beginning? Or had tiny cracks formed that were never patched, allowing huge wedges to form?

She'd likely never know, but it made Maggie think about things in her own life. She had been close to losing that life, frighteningly close, and she began taking a closer look at what was truly important.

Her parents and Joe were truly important to her. Rob was becoming very important to her. But had she treated them as such? When Joe worried about her safety, she had brushed him off with impatience, possibly causing a crack to form. When Rob became hard to reach, instead of understanding the hectic schedules of his work, and allowing for the fact that hers was just as unpredictable, she began to pull back, allowing another little crack to form.

Maggie didn't want wedges to form between her and the people she cared about. It was time to start patching. She reached for the phone.

Maggie hesitated as she held it, wondering who to call first. It should probably be Joe, she thought. After all, he knew the most about what she had been involved in, and he would therefore be the one most worried. He deserved to hear that she was all right, although she would get an earful as he learned what she had gone through. Rob, on the other hand, had been kept in the dark about most of this so far. Therefore, other than perhaps worrying about why he hadn't been able to reach her, he wouldn't be nearly as stressed. Yes, Joe probably should be called first.

Joe or Rob, Rob or Joe. There really shouldn't be a problem, she knew, when it came to choosing between a boyfriend of some months and the brother of one's lifetime. Except, that is, when one could expect a chewing out.

Maggie punched in the familiar numbers.

A chewing out that one knew was deserved. Which, of course, made it all the harder to . . .

The phone clicked, then that familiar baritone voice answered. She drew a breath.

"Rob, I'm so glad I caught you!"